STEPPIN & FAMILY

BY HOPE NEWELL

ILLUSTRATED BY

ANNE MERRIMAN PECK

Cover design by Phillip Colhouer
Cover illustration by Tanya Glebova
Original cover illustration by Anne Merriman Peck
Illustrations by Anne Merriman Peck
First published in 1942
This unabridged version has updated grammar and spelling.
© 2019 Jenny Phillips
www.goodandbeautiful.com

To the One and Only
BILL ROBINSON
with sincere admiration

Table of Contents

CHAPTER 1

Steppin's First
Public Appearance

To see Steppin Stebbins racing down the street one warm afternoon in June, no one would have believed that he was on his way to school. Every other school day in the whole year, it had taken his mother's warning, "You'll be late," and his little sister Mary Ellis' constant scolding to get Steppin through his lunch and back to his desk before the tardy bell rang. But this day was different.

It was the last day of school. No more lessons, no more homework, no more scrambling out of bed in a hurry, nothing but fun for two blessed months! But it was not so much the

thought of freedom to come as the great event of that very afternoon that made Steppin hurry. For he was to do a solo tap
dance at the closing exercises of his class. "My first public appearance," he thought proudly as he ran down the street.

A changing traffic light on Eighth Avenue brought him to an
abrupt halt. Hopping up and down on the curb, Steppin stared
impatiently at the stream of automobiles, trucks, and streetcars
roaring by. The thunder of the elevated trains overhead, the
clank and clatter of streetcars, and the honks of taxis went un-
noticed. His ears were tuned to city din.

"School is out
Hear me shout,"

he crooned under his breath while his feet beat out a tap in the
same rhythm. Brush, brush and hop with his right foot, and
brush, brush and hop with the left foot, over and over. While he
danced, Steppin kept an eye on the green signal. Was it going to
stay that way all day? Wouldn't it ever turn red?

At last it changed, and Steppin darted across the street like
a flash and scurried down the street. Out of habit he looked up
at the street clock, which generally told him he was in danger
of being late. But today he saw that it had taken him only five
minutes to come this far. As school was only two blocks away,
Steppin slowed down to a walk and stopped before his favorite
window, the pawn shop.

Treasures of all kinds were heaped together in the dusty
shop window: guns, tennis rackets, telescopes, banjos, roller
skates, and jack knives. Steppin always played a game before
that window. He picked out the things he would most like to
buy if he had all the money he wanted. He usually spent a long
time over that choice, weighing values carefully. But this day he
paid no attention to the wonderful display. He had caught sight
of his reflection in the gilt mirror that stood at the back of the
showcase.

He eyed himself proudly. "Boy, I sure do look like a professional," he murmured, strutting a little and grinning broadly. His coffee-brown face, shining with the scrubbing he had given it, grinned back at him, showing all of his ivory-white teeth. His hair under the tight skull cap he wore was slicked so close to his skull that it looked as if it was painted on. His big black eyes took in the navy-blue coat of his Sunday suit, the stiffly starched white shirt with a little black bow tie, and the white duck trousers which his friend Charley Kee, the Chinese laundry man, had pressed for him in exchange for errands. Steppin sighed with satisfied approval.

Steppin had pored over the pictures of black celebrities who performed in night clubs and theaters, and this costume was the best imitation of his idols that he could manage. Except for one thing, Steppin was greatly pleased with the elegant entertainer he saw reflected in the mirror. His shoes were all wrong. He had no soft, flexible slippers with metal taps on their tips like a real dancer. He wore a pair of old sneakers and had stuck a cluster of thumb tacks in the tip of each sole to use for taps. They did pretty well, but Steppin was not satisfied with them.

"Oh well, you can't have everything at once, I suppose," he consoled himself. "Anyway, when I get to be a professional, I'm going to have six dozen pairs of dancing shoes at a time, with solid silver taps on every single one of them. Even platinum, maybe, if I want to."

Steppin's dreams of the future carried him happily on to school. A few boys were playing ball in the playground. They called to Steppin to join them. "Not a chance," thought Steppin, not when he was about to make his first public appearance as a dancer. He must keep his clothes in order for an occasion like this. So he entered the large brick building and ran up the stairs to his classroom.

Steppin hardly recognized the familiar room; it looked so festive with garlands of evergreens on the walls and bowls of

flowers on the window sills. Some of the girls who were helping
the teacher, Miss Blair, decorate the room looked festive too,
in their frilly dresses of pink and blue and white, their hair gay
with bows of bright ribbons. Miss Blair herself, in a blue silk
dress, with her blond hair fluffed out around her face, looked as
young as a girl, Steppin thought.

Miss Blair's desk had been taken away, and two big jars of
lilacs stood one on each side of the platform. A bright poster
painted by some of the children served as a backdrop. Steppin
surveyed it with approval. It looked almost like a stage.

But suddenly he thought of the moment when he would
have to step up there before all the boys and girls. Cold shivers
went up his spine. A strange, sinking feeling gripped him in the
stomach. He was scared! Steppin had never thought of that.

"Oh boy, I've got to make good, and here I am as jumpy as a
cat," he thought as he slid into his seat. His own name, Stephen
A. Stebbins, seemed to jump at him from the neatly printed
program on his desk. He stared at it and clenched his clammy
hands under the desk.

While the other boys and girls, demure and solemn in their best
clothes, took their seats, Steppin anxiously went over in his mind
the dance routine he had so carefully worked out. He counted out
the steps to the tune of "Marching Through Georgia" which his
sister, Mary Ellis, was to play for his accompaniment. Brush, brush
and hop; and brush, brush and hop; heel and toe and break. "Gee,
I'd like to have a tune with some snap to it," he thought. But the few
selections which Mary Ellis could play by ear on the wheezy old
organ at home did not include pieces with snap.

In a daze, Steppin heard Miss Blair make her little opening
speech and then announce: "And now we will have the first
number on our program, a recitation of Kipling's poem *If* by
Martin Burns, Junior." Martin had been speaking that piece
on every school program since he was in the fourth grade, and
never yet had he been able to get through all the "ifs" without

help. Steppin had never before felt the slightest interest in his struggles, but now he found himself waiting in an agony of suspense every time Martin hesitated. When for the fourth time he began "If you can" and stopped, open mouthed, with imploring eyes fixed on Miss Blair, Steppin knew how he felt. Suppose I forget my dance steps! But Miss Blair, with whispered prompting, urged Martin on to the final line which he knew by heart and which he spoke in ringing, triumphant tones. "AND WHAT IS MORE, YOU'LL BE A MAN, MY SON."

Steppin's place was fifth on the program. It had seemed a long way down the list, but now the time was coming, quickly, surely, when he would have to get up on the platform and dance. He saw Mary Ellis come in quietly and take a seat. She had been excused early from her class so that she might play for him. Oh, if only something had happened to keep her from coming! But there she was, smiling at him as calmly as though he were not crazy with stage fright and about to be disgraced before the whole school.

The sweet, clear notes of a cornet recalled Steppin from his miserable thoughts. That was David Harmon, and he was playing the Schubert Serenade. David played in the school orchestra and was an old hand at public appearances. Watching him standing there so easy and calm, Steppin felt sick with envy and fright. "I would have to be billed next to him," he thought unhappily. "Oh boy, why didn't I practice more on cartwheels, so I could do a cartwheel, then go into a split to finish the act? I could try, maybe, but like as not I'd land on my head and a fine finale that would be."

The last soft note of the Serenade died away. David bowed gracefully and returned to his seat. "That was lovely, David." Miss Blair rose and beamed on him; then, still smiling, she glanced kindly at Steppin. "The next number will be a tap dance by Stephen A. Stebbins, and"—she smiled at Mary Ellis—"his little sister will play his accompaniment."

Like one in a dream, Steppin found himself getting to his feet, while before him the big yellow bow on Mary Ellis' hair bobbed up as she rose and went to the piano. His knees trembled, but somehow he mounted the platform and bowed gravely. This wasn't a bit the way he had dreamed it—this horrible nightmare. But there was nothing to do about it, nothing to do but dance. Mary Ellis struck the first chord. To his surprise his feet responded, although they felt like solid blocks of wood. Mechanically he went through the simple steps of his dance. In a few moments, he forgot the staring boys and girls in front of him and began to dance as though his life depended on it. He thought of nothing but the rhythm and the beat of his dancing feet. He varied his few steps with pantomime, making himself very tall, then letting his arms hang perfectly limp from his shoulders so that they flapped queerly with every step. Someone giggled. Then a chuckle swept over the room. That did it. It was all fun now. Joyously he hopped and whirled. No longer afraid, he varied his pantomime, now grinning at his audience, now looking very solemn.

He had just completed a quick whirl on one foot and was finishing with a split when he felt a stinging in the soles of his feet. Steppin knew very well what that meant. The thumbtacks were working through the soles of his shoes! Every time he hopped the pain grew worse. Brush, brush, tap; brush, brush, tap, ouch! Steppin nearly yelled out with pain. "I can't give up; the show has got to go on," he reminded himself, like an old trouper. And all the while his feet tapped, and his face wore a stiff, frozen smile.

Then one of the boys began clapping in time to the music. Soon others joined in, marking the beat. "Boy, they're with me. I got to go on if it kills me." Steppin flashed his white teeth in a bright, agonized grin and spread out his hands in an inviting gesture to his friends. The whole room broke into clapping. "Almost over now," thought Steppin. Mary Ellis was pounding out the last chorus—"Hurrah, hurrah, the flag that makes us free."

Suddenly Steppin tripped! The thumbtacks in his shoes had

caught on a rough spot of the floor. Quick as a flash, even as he stumbled, Steppin knew there was only one thing to do. He threw out his arms and, hurling himself forward with all his might, tried to turn his fall into a cartwheel. He felt himself flying through space, and in the next instant he was teetering on his feet, gasping for breath as he slid to the floor in a fast split.

In a daze he heard the loud applause, and suddenly he realized that in his cartwheel he had flung himself right off the platform. A pleased grin spread from ear to ear. "Well, tie my shoes! I didn't know I had it in me."

Just then, Mary Ellis, who had gone placidly on with her piece, struck the last chord with a resounding thump. Steppin scrambled to his feet, bowed politely as Miss Blair had taught him, and limped to his seat. The continued clapping was music in his ears. He looked over at Miss Blair, who smiled and nodded encouragingly. Steppin rose and bowed again with a flourish, glowing with pride and happiness.

The program continued, but Steppin hardly heard or saw what was going on, though he clapped heartily for each performer. He was lost in a haze of glory and triumph. "Boy, applause sure is jam on my bread," he chuckled while he slyly removed the torturing thumbtacks from his shoes. "From now on, nothing is going to stop me. I'm going to be a first-class dancer or bust."

CHAPTER 2

Service with a Smile

"Last call for breakfast."

Steppin had just walked out from the wings and was stepping up to the footlights in response to a tremendous burst of applause from his audience, when his mother's voice calling him from the kitchen interrupted his dream of having become a famous dancer.

He flopped over in bed and half-opened his eyes.

"Well anyway, it's Saturday, and I don't have to go to school," he cheered himself as the beautiful dream faded away. And then with a thrill of pleasure he remembered: "It's vacation." He closed his eyes again.

"Each and every day is Saturday from now on," he gloated,

"every single day except Sunday, and Sunday School doesn't even start until eleven."

For a few minutes he lay buried in the covers, reveling in his good fortune. Then suddenly, wide awake, he became absorbed in the delightful task of making plans for the summer.

"Boy, am I going to be busy!" He raised himself on one elbow and snapped his fingers. "First off, I got to earn some money so I can take a course at the Elite Dancing School, then I got to find me a job as a dancer, and next I got to see about joining the H.D.A. gang.

"Goodness, it's too bad I wasn't born triplets. Maybe I could get something done then. One of me could go to school and help Mom with the janitor work and all like that. Then another one of me could take care of my dancing career, and then the third one could just mess around having a good time. That would be a swell idea all right, just so I wasn't the one that had to go to school."

Before he could decide just which one of the triplets would be Steppin A. Stebbins, he was interrupted by his mother frowning at him from the doorway.

"Steppin, I'm pouring the last of the batter on the griddle, and if you want any breakfast you'd better march yourself out here," she scolded.

As she opened the door, a tantalizing odor of salt pork frying and griddle cakes browning whiffed in at him, causing a sharp, hollow pang in his stomach. In an instant he forgot everything except that he was starving.

"I'm coming," he shouted.

"You'd better," threatened Mrs. Stebbins, "because in about two minutes I'm going to begin clearing up."

Steppin bounded out of bed as if a bomb had exploded under it. He struggled into his faded blue bathrobe and, thrusting his toes into his felt house slippers, he shuffled out to the kitchen.

The Stebbins family lived in what is known as a railroad flat, but a "train of cars flat" would have been a better name for it. The rooms were in one long line with doors opening into each other, just like the cars of a train. They called the rooms coaches, and Mary Ellis had given each coach a name taken from a book of poems she was always reading.

Steppin flopped his way out of his room which was called the "Casa Bianca," then through Mary Ellis' room, the "Anabel Lee," and on through the extra room, which, since it served as a storage space for hats, coats, rubbers, toys, and whatnot, was appropriately called "The Wreck of the Hesperus."

When he reached the kitchen, he found that his mother really had begun to clear up.

"Your cakes will be ready to lift by the time you have washed," she told him. "You can help yourself."

After vigorously sousing his face and head in cold water under the tap of the set tub, Steppin stacked six large wheat cakes on his plate and helped himself to the sliced salt pork which had been dipped in cornmeal and fried to a beautiful golden crisp.

The dining car, to which Steppin now proceeded, made the house seem more like a train than ever. It was just a corner of the kitchen with two windows looking out into the backyard, but some former tenant had installed a real Pullman dining table and two genuine cane-covered coach seats in it.

Steppin sat down and slid himself over to the window. In one corner of the yard was a little shed which the children called the caboose. As his mother was superintendent of the apartment house, the Stebbins family lived in the basement and had the use of the backyard and the shed. It was on condition that Mrs. Stebbins would permit the H.D.A. gang to use the shed for a clubhouse, that Snakey Lewis had promised to persuade the gang leader to have Steppin initiated as a member.

As Steppin was eating, he kept speculating on his chances of getting his mother's consent to let the H.D.A. members occupy the shed. Mrs. Stebbins had her own opinion of Snakey Lewis and of Butch Weldon, who was captain of the gang. Although Steppin had assured Snakey that his mother would have no objections, he felt far from sure of winning her over now that he was about to bring up the subject. He decided he had better work up to it gradually.

"Where is Pedigree, Mom?" he asked pleasantly.

"I loaned him to Mrs. Mack," Mrs. Stebbins replied. "She has been bothered with rats."

"He won't be gone long," Steppin prophesied. "That dog sure is rough on rats."

"He sure is," his mother agreed.

Steppin was just about to introduce the subject of his promotion to Junior High as a pleasant topic of conversation when he became aware of a clear young voice calling from the caboose.

"Mary Ellis, would you kindly sweep off this carpet, please?"

Steppin recognized the speaker as Virginia Day, his sister's inseparable companion. He leaned out of the window to get a better view of the shed. Mary Ellis was industriously sweeping a scrap of old carpet in the yard while Virginia was sweeping out the shed.

"Mom, what are Virginia and Mary Ellis doing to that caboose?" he demanded.

"They are going to clean it up and use it for a playhouse." Mrs. Stebbins calmly emptied and dried the dishpan, quite unaware that her matter-of-fact answer was a great blow to her only son.

"A playhouse!" Steppin nearly choked with indignation.

"Have you any objections?" Mrs. Stebbins asked mildly.

"I sure have!" Steppin dropped his spoon with a clatter. "I and some of the boys want that shed for a clubhouse."

"A clubhouse!" Mrs. Stebbins hung the dishcloth on a nail and turned around. "I suppose you mean a place for Bertrand Weldon and those other young hooligans to come and raise a rumpus all day."

"We wouldn't raise a rumpus all day, Mom, we just want a nice, quiet place where we can hold our meetings."

"No indeed, sir! In the first place, I've already promised it to Mary Ellis, and in the second place, I wouldn't even *think* of letting that good-for-nothing gang congregate in my backyard, annoying the tenants, to say nothing of driving me insane!"

"Ah, but Mom—"

"Steppin, please don't trouble me about it anymore. It's bad enough to have you associating with such rowdies on the streets without bringing them home."

Poor Steppin! It was as if a dark cloud had suddenly blotted out the sun. He knew there was no use arguing with his mother when she took that tone. What would Snakey think of him? If only he hadn't been so positive when he promised Snakey they could use the shed!

"Step-pin! Hey Step-pin," a shrill voice was shouting from the outside hallway.

That was Snakey now! Steppin quickly decided he had better have a little time to think up excuses before they met. He got up from the table and, sneaking back to his room, hurriedly dressed. Then he quietly slipped out of the back door without bothering to speak to the two young ladies who had so innocently caused his present trouble. Steppin scrambled over the backyard fence and, by walking through an areaway, presently emerged on Strivers Row.

Some of the wealthiest people in Harlem lived on Strivers Row. The wide, tree-lined street with its beautiful houses always fascinated Steppin, and the minute he stepped from the areaway into the bright sunshine, his spirits began to rise. For the time, he forgot all about Snakey Lewis and the H.D.A. gang.

As he strolled along to Seventh Avenue, Steppin read the brass name plates of prosperous doctors and lawyers who had their offices in this famous block. One very beautiful yellow brick house with wide balustrades and quaintly carved steps was boarded up. "For Sale or Rent," a placard read.

"Someday I'm going to buy that place and nail up a big brass sign with

STEPPIN STEBBINS, DANCER
AND FAMILY

engraved on it," he promised himself.

When Steppin reached the wide stretch of green grass and trees that runs through the middle of Seventh Avenue, he sat down on the high cement curb and took a worn and very dirty yellow envelope out of his hip pocket. In the envelope was a paper folder marked "Postal Savings," a smudgy piece of cardboard with six postal savings stamps pasted on it, and a stubby bit of pencil. Steppin pushed his blue and yellow skull cap off his forehead and studied his assets.

"I got one dollar on deposit and sixty cents in stamps. The dance course costs five dollars, so before I even begin to take lessons, I'll have to earn—let me see—" here Steppin scowled heavily and began to figure on the back of the envelope. "I'll have to earn three dollars and forty cents."

He put the envelope carefully away and rose to his feet with a sigh.

"Well, I expect I'd better get to work."

Steppin's first destination was a dingy little shop in a basement on West 135th Street. The counters were stacked high with great piles of heavy brown paper shopping bags with strong rope handles. The place was full of young black boys and girls who were noisily engaged in buying the bags from "Pops," the elderly proprietor.

"I'll take twenty plain bags and five with pictures on them," Steppin ordered when his turn came. "I might be back for more later."

"You may save yourself a long walk if you take more now," the old man urged, but Steppin was firm.

"Nope, I got to see how these go before I tie up any more of my money."

He hung his stock of bags on a wire hoop attached to his belt and hurried along the long crosstown blocks to the great street market on Park Avenue. Up and down the middle of the avenue, under the elevated structure, push carts were parked in a double line, heaped with goods of all kinds. Over the piles of fruit and vegetables and the displays of gleaming fish, hawkers leaned, shouting loudly at the jostling women shoppers. One man cried the cheapness of his cartful of snails—lively merchandise which kept escaping down the orderly piles in which he put them. Rubber balloons in weird shapes and colors swung from racks next to rows of cheap, gaudy dresses and carts piled with hats and shoes.

Steppin plunged into the bustling confusion, darting in and out between bargain hunters, competing with dozens of other boys and girls who were all trying to sell their bags. He caught sight of an anxious-faced Irish woman whom he spotted as a likely customer. Her shabby hat was tipped over one eye, and wisps of bright red hair were hanging in her face. She was fairly puffing with the effort of trying to carry several bundles in one hand, while she clutched the hand of a tired, cross little boy with the other.

"Shopping bag, lady? Only three cents. Save you trouble!"

Steppin flashed a bright smile at her and shook open a bag with one grand flourish. The woman looked wistfully into the tempting emptiness of the bag.

"Yes, I guess I had better buy one," she sighed.

Steppin helped her transfer her packages into the bag and held it while she fished the pennies from her purse.

"There now, isn't that better?"

"It sure is, sonny." The woman returned his friendly smile as she took the bag and went on.

"Service with a smile—that's what gets them," Steppin decided as he settled down to a day's work.

Business was pretty good, and in about two hours, Steppin had sold all but two bags. His next customer was a very fussy, grim-looking woman who couldn't seem to make up her mind just how she wished to arrange her parcels. First, she decided to put a box of eggs in the bottom of the bag, and then when Steppin had helped her pack in the other things, she insisted upon taking everything out and repacking the bag with the eggs on top.

"There you are, madam," Steppin said pleasantly when everything was arranged to her satisfaction. "Three cents, please."

"Three cents!" the woman fairly shrieked at him. "What kind of racket is this? I never paid more than two cents at any of the stores!"

"Yeah, but you're a long way from a store, missus," Steppin drawled. "You see, I pay two cents for the bags myself. The other penny is for service and like that."

"Service indeed! Highway robbery, I call it. Why, I never heard of such an outrage. I'll pay two cents and not a penny more."

The woman thrust two pennies under Steppin's nose. "If you don't want to take these you can just unpack that bag and give me the parcels."

Steppin pocketed the pennies and then drew himself up proudly.

"Lady, I wouldn't unpack that bag again for a dollar." He waved his hand emphatically. "It's all yours."

The woman sniffed and tossed her head, and then with a final triumphant smirk, she strode off. Steppin drew the back of his hand across his forehead and then shook it as if he were wiping away beads of perspiration.

"Phew, what a rip off! A half-hour's work and all my profit shot to pieces."

"Here, boy," a brisk, impatient voice interrupted his reflections.

"Another tough customer," Steppin thought. "Oh well, service with a smile—that's Steppin A. Stebbins."

He turned and smiled sourly at the large, red-faced woman who glared back at him.

"Don't stand there grinning like a jack-o-lantern. Can't you see I'm in a hurry?"

Before Steppin could open the bag, she began piling bundles in his arms.

"There, now follow me to my car," she commanded.

With his recent unpleasant encounter so fresh in his thoughts, Steppin was of half a mind to refuse. However, as the woman was already some distance ahead of him, he decided he might as well see it through. He followed her sturdy, well-shined brown oxfords as she strode through the crowds to a side street where a long, low robin's-egg-blue roadster with glittering nickel trimmings was drawn up to the curb.

"Don't bother with the bag, just dump everything in here," she ordered, raising the top of the rumble seat.

By the time Steppin had disposed of the parcels, the woman had taken her seat behind the wheel and banged the car door. She handed him a fifty-cent piece over the back of the seat.

Steppin started going through his pockets for change.

"Have you anything smaller?" he started to ask when, with a horrible shriek of grinding gears and a terrific lurch, the car shot away.

For a minute, Steppin stood with his mouth open, staring after the car. It was only when it had passed the intersection and vanished that he began to realize his good fortune.

"Can you tie that! One customer cheats you out of a penny after she gets a half-hour's work out of you, and the next one gives you fifty cents for almost nothing."

Steppin shook his head in amazement.

"Oh well, I always say, you never know what life holds for you," he thought.

[HAPTER 3

Introducing Mr. Kee, Pedigree, and Snakey

It was nearly three o'clock when Steppin reached home. Racing down the steep cement steps to the basement, he was hailed by Mr. Charley Kee from his laundry, which was just next door and also below the street level.

"Hi, you Steppin. Your mama went to buy dinner—she left your key here."

"Some hot!" was Mr. Kee's greeting as Steppin dashed into the steamy little laundry. His slanting almond eyes twinkled pleasantly behind his steel-rimmed spectacles.

"It sure is," agreed Steppin.

"Pedigree is in a hurry to see you," went on Mr. Kee, nodding toward the Stebbins' apartment from which an uproarious barking and scratching of dog feet could be heard.

"I'll say!" Steppin grinned as he took a large key labeled "super" from a nail on the door casing.

Often Steppin lingered in Charley's shop, perched on one of the high wooden stools, talking while he watched, fascinated by the quick, sure movements of the little Chinese laundry man as he sprinkled, ironed, and folded shirts at lightning speed. But today Steppin was much too hungry to wait longer for his lunch.

"So long and thanks for the key," he said and scampered up the steps.

As he opened the door of his home, Pedigree rushed at him barking joyously, his tan and yellow body quivering and his long, drooping ears flapping. Pedigree was a curious mixture of hound and wire-haired terrier, and, as Steppin said, his two breeds never mixed. Now his rough, springy, wire-haired coat, bristled and erect, remained, as usual, only at half-mast. He had the quick, alert movements of a terrier, but his eyes, even in this moment of joy, were the soft-brown, mournful eyes of a hound. The tail was unusually long, even for a hound, and curved so that it barely cleared the floor as Pedigree wagged it furiously.

Steppin had named him Pedigree when he was a puppy because he had once heard a man speak of a dog as having a long pedigree, and he thought that a dog's tail and his pedigree were one and the same thing.

After a few moments of joyous greeting, Pedigree, who was rather tired from his morning of rat chasing, settled down on the floor. With his forepaws tucked under his wet chin, he watched Steppin with sad but eager eyes as he ate lunch.

"As soon as I finish eating, I'm going to mosey right over and buy another lot of bags," Steppin promised himself. But after he had put away three bowls of vegetable soup, six slices of bread and butter, a glass of milk, two doughnuts, and a dill pickle, he began to feel less and less inclined to work.

"Do you know sumpin'?" Steppin prodded Pedigree gently with his foot. "I'm half of a mind to call it a day and take you for a nice run in the park."

Upon hearing the word "park," Pedigree bounded at Steppin, almost knocking him over, chair and all. Then, as if he feared that even his wild demonstration might not convey to his master his complete approval of this plan, he trotted into The Wreck of the Hesperus and returned carrying his leash in his mouth.

As soon as they were out of the house, Pedigree started on a dead run for the park, but much to his disgust, Steppin, after a brief struggle, began dragging him in the opposite direction. Steppin had wisely decided to deposit some of his earnings, for he knew from experience that the less money he kept in his pocket, the less he would be tempted to spend.

"Two dollars in the bank and eighty-five cents over to buy bags!" Steppin felt quite wealthy as he stepped away from the Postal Savings window of the branch post office. Less than three more dollars to earn, and then he would be able to take the course in dancing that would surely make him a professional. Steppin never for a moment doubted but that he would be a first-class dancer when he had completed the course. Countless times he had studied the advertisement in the Harlem newspaper which read:

ELITE DANCING SCHOOL
Ten Lessons for Five Dollars
Guaranteed Course
Professional Engagements Secured for Our Graduates

There it was in black and white. As soon as he completed the course, his career would begin.

With Pedigree tugging at the leash and dragging him on toward the park, Steppin planned his bright future. After his long morning at the market, he found it very pleasant to sit propped against a tree trunk on the cool grass. He unleashed Pedigree, who bounded off, returning immediately with a stick for Steppin to throw for him. While he kept Pedigree busy retrieving sticks, Steppin fell to dreaming of the time when, as a great tap dancer, his name would become a household word in Harlem. As he watched children in little groups roller-skating, playing ball, jumping rope, and playing hopscotch on the chalk-marked cement paths, he thought:

"Some day when I'm sittin' here in this park, they will all be noticing me. 'That's Steppin Stebbins, the famous dancer,' they will be saying to each other. I expect they will be pestering me for autographs." He smiled complacently.

From his pocket he took a pencil and envelope and began practicing writing autographs while Pedigree lay at his feet panting contentedly.

> "To my true friend, Snakey Lewis."
> "To David Harmon, from his great admirer."
> "With best good wishes to Martin Burns."

and so on. After each inscription he signed his name Steppin A. Stebbins in large, round letters.

By the time he had so honored all his school friends, the long shadows of late afternoon were falling across the park. Children were gathering up their toys, noisily shouting their farewells, and there was a regular procession of mothers and baby carriages filing through the park exits.

Steppin was beginning to think of supper when he heard a bell jangling and a shrill voice calling:

"Hot sweet potatoes! Three for ten. Take them away."

The warm, delicious odor of roasted sweet potatoes preceded Old John, the potato man, as he wheeled his little charcoal oven toward Steppin. The boy's fingers crept into his pocket and clutched the coins he had kept. Baked sweet potatoes were one of Steppin's favorite treats, and his mother never had them in summer because she cooked on a gas plate which had no oven. Indeed, it was surprising to find Old John selling them so late in the season, for he usually changed his wares from potatoes and roasted chestnuts to ices and cold drinks in warm weather. It seemed to Steppin extraordinary that Old John should be selling roast potatoes at supper time and that he, Steppin, should have sufficient money in his pocket to buy them.

"I could spend ten cents and still have plenty left for capital," he tempted himself. "Nope." Reluctantly he let the coin slip from his long brown fingers and withdrew his hand from his pocket. "If I'm ever going to amount to anything, I'll just have to beware of temptations like this."

He quickly snapped the leash on Pedigree's collar, and holding his breath for fear the tantalizing odor of the potatoes might weaken his determination, he ran by Old John and his charcoal stove and started for home. He had walked hardly a block when he saw the well-known figure of Snakey Lewis ambling toward him.

"Boy! Now I am in a fix." Steppin tugged on Pedigree's leash and slowed down to a crawl to temporarily delay this most unwelcome meeting.

"I should have been cooking up something to tell Snakey instead of loafing in the park planning my future. Now I sure got to think fast to explain why I can't let the gang use the shed like I promised."

Steppin knew all too well that it would never do to give the truthful explanation that his mother had refused to let the gang use the shed. He could not stand the humiliation of admitting to Snakey that he was just talking through his hat when he had so glibly offered it. Besides, there was Snakey's gang, the H.D.A., to be reckoned with. Did not each member wear a red-and-green cotton grocer's cap with the letters H.D.A. printed over the visor? These caps were distributed free by a local grocer, and the letters really stood for Home Dairy Association. But woe to any non-member who dared to flaunt one, for to Steppin and to every other boy in the neighborhood, the caps were the official emblem of the gang, and the menacing letters stood for Harlem's Dread Avengers.

"Hi, Snakey! How you doin'?" Steppin said in an off-hand way.

"I'm doin' all right. How're you?"

"Oh, just hangin' together, about." Steppin's tone suggested that he was a world-weary traveler on the way to a long-post-poned rest. "Maybe I can just ease by and not say anything about the shed," he thought hopefully.

But Snakey stopped dead and plunged at once into the one topic which Steppin did not want to discuss.

"Say, Steppin, I been talkin' to the gang, and I think I got it all fixed up about your joining. It was pretty hard to get them around to letting you in—you see Butch kind of held off on account of your mother being so strict, but I finally put it over."

Snakey was enjoying his position as goodwill ambassador between the gang and Steppin. It was very seldom that he had a chance to appear important. In fact, his only social gift, and the chief reason that he, himself, had been accepted by the gang, was his amazing feat of being able to kick the back of his head with both feet at once.

"Gee, that's great." Steppin stretched his dry lips in what he hoped was an enthusiastic smile.

"I knew you'd be pleased as pie." Snakey's voice was hoarse with excitement. "They're goin' to initiate you at the next meeting, and Butch is all set to have it in your shed."

"It sure was great of you to fix things up for me, but you see, I can't join up just yet."

Snakey's mouth dropped open.

"Well, it's like this, Snakey. Of course I want to join in the worst kind of way, but just now I'm so busy I don't know which way to turn. You see, I'm trying to earn some money, so I can get started on my dancing career. Then when I get some money, I'll be spending all my time learning some dance routines from a professional. The fact is, what with practicing and all, I don't think I'll have any time to spare for a couple of months."

"A couple of months!" Snakey's face was a picture of dismay. "Gee, Steppin, I don't know what I'm goin' to tell Butch. He's so dead set on using that shed. Maybe your mother would let us use it anyway?" Snakey asked hopefully.

"I could ask her," Steppin said obligingly. "But I don't think she would want a lot of strange kids on the premises unless I was there to look after things."

"Well, you will ask her, won't you?" Snakey pleaded.

As Steppin was quick to observe, Snakey had dropped the pretense that he was urging the gang to accept Steppin as a member. All Snakey's swaggering self-confidence had left him. His voice was eager, almost beseeching.

"Sure, I'll do my best," Steppin promised. "But I don't think she'll be agreeable. I guess she is pretty strict, like you said."

"Ask her right away tonight, won't you Steppin? And I'll hold off telling the gang—and Butch—until I hear."

Snakey actually winced as he mentioned Butch's name. It came over Steppin in a flash that Snakey was just plain scared.

"After all, I'm only in bad with him, and he's got Butch to settle with," Steppin thought. And a feeling of relief rushed over him like a wave. He was just about to bid Snakey farewell when he heard the tinkle of the bell and the familiar cry, "Red hot potatoes! Three for ten." An inspiration seized him.

"Say, Snakey, would you grant me the loan of your shoeshine box for a few minutes?"

"Sure thing, Step. I'd just as gladly you took it as not."

Steppin could hardly believe his ears. Boys who had shoeshine boxes were seldom willing to loan them. In fact, it was considered poor taste to ask for one. Steppin knew now that, until he gave his final decision in regard to the shed, he had Snakey completely in his power.

"Thanks a lot. And say, could I trouble you to take Pedigree home with you? I can pick him up when I bring back the box."

"No trouble at all," Snakey assured him.

As soon as the exchange was made, Steppin hurried to a corner where home-coming workers were pouring out of the subway exit.

> "I got a head
> And I got feet
> A man like me is hard to beat."

He tapped and hummed modestly as he waited for customers.

"Shine, Mister?" he interrupted himself to call eagerly, whenever a good prospect passed. Good fortune was with him; he caught two customers almost immediately. Then following the sound of the bell, he overtook Old John and exchanged the two nickels he had earned for the coveted potatoes.

Mrs. Stebbins and Mary Ellis were just about to sit down to supper when Steppin and Pedigree dashed into the kitchen.

"Look, Mom!" Steppin opened his newspaper package and dumped the three piping hot, roasted potatoes on the table.

"Oh, Mom," exclaimed Mary Ellis, "sweet potatoes! Ain't that sumpin'? I'll make salad out of the white potatoes, and we can have them tomorrow night."

Mrs. Stebbins shook her head.

"Steppin, sometimes I just don't know what to do about you. Here I was all worked up to give you a good scolding for staying out so late, and now what can I say? I might have known you'd be all right, though," she added kindly. "You're thoughtless, goodness knows, but you always mean well. You're a sweet child in spite of all your mischief, and you're smart too. You favor your father in that."

Steppin's brown face shone with pleasure. To be told that he resembled his dead father whom he could not even remember was the highest praise his mother could give him.

He sighed contentedly as he mashed a huge sweet potato with his fork and arranged a small lake of gravy in the middle of it. On the whole, his first day of vacation had been a huge success.

CHAPTER 4

Steppin Tries to Make a Bargain

"Three days raining, not counting Sunday. I don't suppose it's ever going to stop!"

Steppin let go of the huge ash can he and High Pockets were carrying and stood staring through the grating of the basement entrance to the house.

"Iffen it never stops, there's no call for you to drop a whole can of ashes on my feet almost," High Pockets grumbled.

Without answering, Steppin continued to stare at the rain pelting into the cement areaway.

"Well, are you goin' to help me carry out the ash cans, or are you aiming to stop here makin' a general inspection of nothing all day?" High Pockets demanded.

Steppin reluctantly followed the enormously tall handyman back to the furnace room to collect the last of the ash cans and carry it out to the street.

"I guess if you saw your business going to ruin on account of this rain you wouldn't be calling it nothing," Steppin grumbled as they took hold of the can and dragged it out into the long hall.

"Here it is Thursday, and I've hardly taken in a dollar since last Saturday," Steppin reflected bitterly as he grunted with the exertion of half-dragging and half-lifting the ash can. "Summer will be practically over before I get enough money to take dancing lessons. If I could only get the five dollars, I could maybe learn a new dance every day for a week, and then I'd be all set for a job. Maybe if I get a real good dancing job, Mom wouldn't make me go to school. Maybe—"

Steppin stopped short just as he and High Pockets had half-lifted the can up the step leading to the areaway. He let his end drop with a bang, and heedless of High Pockets' complaints, he raced through the house and into his room.

A great idea had struck Steppin—a magnificent and daring idea. As if the weight of it was too overpowering to be supported standing up, Steppin threw himself down on his bed.

"Maybe I could pay the school what I have saved and ask them to trust me for the rest. Especially since they promise to get me a job. I could pay them out of my first week's salary. Hot diggity, I wonder why I never thought of that before."

For a few minutes, Steppin lay with his chin propped in his hand, overwhelmed by his own genius. Then, in a daze, he got up and went out to the kitchen where his mother and Mary Ellis had prepared lunch. During the meal he was so preoccupied that he not only did not resent, but hardly heard, Mary Ellis' excited chatter about the furnishing of the caboose, to which she and Virginia were devoting every spare minute.

When he buttered a third slice of bread and piled it on top of the two other slices he hadn't eaten, Mrs. Stebbins and Mary Ellis smiled at each other.

"Wool gathering." Mary Ellis framed the words with her mouth, and Mrs. Stebbins nodded. Steppin's fits of absent-mindedness were a source of considerable amusement to his womenfolk. When lunch was over, Steppin further astonished them by taking down the dish pan and clearing the table. This was almost too much for Mary Ellis, as it was her turn to wash dishes. She had to rush out to the backyard to keep from giggling right then and there. Mrs. Stebbins, who was almost as near to laughter as her daughter, hurried off to check up on the indolent High Pockets, who was languidly mopping the hallways and stairs.

Meanwhile, Steppin finished his self-appointed chore in half the time it usually took him. Then, after ducking his head under the faucet and plastering down his hair, he went to his room and dressed himself carefully in his best blue coat and white duck pants. Next, he unearthed an ancient black cotton umbrella from The Wreck of the Hesperus, and after making sure that Pedigree was shut in the backyard, he slipped out through the front door.

As he trudged along in the rain, Steppin tried to visualize the interior of the Elite Dancing School, which he had studied so often from the outside. At the same time, he began to plan just what he would say when he got there.

"Sir, my name is Steppin A. Stebbins. I have a little business proposition I would like to talk over with you—"

"Sir, could you give me a few minutes of your time, so I could tell you about a plan of mine which would be of mutual benefit to the both of us?"

The whole idea had seemed as easy as pie when he first thought of it, but now it struck Steppin that the first few minutes would be pretty hard going.

"Maybe it would be better to write a letter than to just walk in and put it up to the school, cold," he wavered. "But if I did that, I wouldn't hear from them for a couple of days at least."

Steppin had stopped and was staring idly at a shop window. His mind was so taken up with the Elite Dancing School that it was some time before the amazing collection of merchandise in front of him became visible to his eyes. Trays of small ivory elephants and tiny coral hands with crossed fingers, finger rings and dozens of other varieties of "lucky" tokens were displayed in the window.

Steppin was especially intrigued by a card placed before a tray of mounted rabbits' feet that read: "Buy a rabbit's foot and carry your luck with you. Only 25¢."

"Boy, I sure would like some luck to carry with me," he murmured, and without a moment's hesitation he entered the shop.

A bell tinkled in the rear of the building as Steppin closed the door behind him. The shop was empty of customers and very dark. Steppin walked around, looking at its fascinating objects. A large cage of white rats caught and held his attention. Another card read: "Lucky white rats. Only 50 cents."

Steppin poked his finger through the wires and touched the quivering pink nose of one of them.

"Maybe a rat would be even better than a rabbit's foot," he thought. Hearing a deep voice behind him, Steppin turned with a start and jerked his finger out of the cage. At sight of the shopkeeper, his jaw dropped and his eyes opened until there was as much white showing as there was brown.

The shopkeeper was a tall, very black and sleek-looking man, wearing a high-necked purple tunic with a wide sash tied around the waist. His hair was completely concealed in yards and yards of bright-yellow silk which was wound around his head like a turban.

"I see you are interested in the white rats," the storekeeper said briskly.

"But how could I carry him?" he asked of the shopkeeper, fingering the money in his pocket.

"Oh, that's easy." The shopkeeper picked up a little wicker cage, popped one of the rats into it, and handed it to Steppin. "There you are, young man, the finest 'luck piece' in the world, complete with cage, only seventy-five cents."

"Seventy-five cents!"

Steppin half-started to put the money back in his pocket again, but the man seemed so confident and so overpowering that Steppin weakened. He handed over three quarters in exchange for the rat and silently walked out of the shop.

"Well, the rat will be a nice pet, anyway," he excused his weakness.

ELITE DANCING SCHOOL

As Steppin stood and read the familiar sign, he felt his heart pounding. At last he was on the verge of his great adventure. A painted wooden hand attached to the sign pointed up to the second floor. Steppin stepped into the narrow hall and slowly climbed the bare, creaky stairs. There, music from a badly tuned piano could be heard coming from behind a door. Beneath the name of the school was a "walk in" sign. Steppin drew a long breath and opened the door.

Afterward he could not have said what he expected to find on the other side of the door. But what he did find surprised him so that for a moment he could only stand and stare. The room had no furniture except a couple of benches and a few plain chairs against one wall and a large mirror at the far end. There was an upright piano at the end near Steppin. Seated at the piano was a very large black woman wearing a bright-red dress.

Against the opposite wall, a bar about four feet from the floor stretched the length of the room. Standing at intervals along this bar and facing the mirror was a line of girls. All of them were dressed in rompers and socks like babies. A woman teacher stood in the center of the room, directing the girls who were doing exercises in time with the music.

Girls! Steppin had never imagined a class of girls and a woman teacher. Fortunately, as he stood behind the piano, he was not visible to anyone in the room, even though they were all staring into the mirror.

"Whoever heard of learning dancing by hanging onto a railing and doing silly exercises?" Steppin snorted indignantly. "Besides, I've got to have a man teacher."

He was just about to slip out when he heard the patter and scratching of small feet coming up the stairs. Then the door was pushed open, and with a shrill bark of triumph, Pedigree dashed into the room and rushed at him. The music stopped abruptly, and Steppin felt himself the center of attention.

"Down, Pedigree! Down, I say!" Steppin commanded.

But then Pedigree's sharp nose caught a scent that none of his tribe had ever ignored. With a growl of rage, he leaped high and dashed the little wicker cage from Steppin's hand. Steppin tried to ward off the dog with his umbrella while he grabbed for the cage, but Pedigree was too quick for him. Like a flash, he pounced upon the flimsy cage, and in an instant a tiny, terrified, white rat was fleeing down the room with Pedigree barking and snarling as he scampered after him. At the sight of the rat, bedlam broke loose in the Elite Dancing School.

"Help! Help!" girls screamed and shrieked while they fell over each other in a mad dash for safety. Steppin had an impression of innumerable bare brown legs climbing on benches, on the window sills, and even on the piano.

"It's that boy—he did it." He heard a voice shrill above the general din.

Steppin felt completely helpless. Even if he could have made himself heard, he despaired of calling Pedigree from the chase. The noise and confusion had added to the dog's excitement. Round and round the room he ran, knocking over chairs, blind to everything but his prey.

Steppin was just about to desert the two animals and sneak off when the rat, after a flying leap over his feet, took refuge under the piano.

"I'll go for a cop," he heard someone shout as he threw himself on the floor and rescued the rat. He thrust the miserable little creature into his pocket and, dashing out of the room, clattered down the stairs with Pedigree barking at his heels. Until he was around the corner and halfway up the next block, Steppin ran at top speed. Then he glanced behind him and, seeing that no one was following, stopped and took a deep breath.

"Whew!" he exhaled noisily, "What a mess I'm in now."

Pedigree, still wild with excitement, began leaping at the pocket in which Steppin was still clutching the rat.

"You mutt!" Steppin shook his umbrella at the dog. "You better get out of here before I get any madder."

A rat, and he was not to be permitted to chase it? Pedigree let his long tail droop between his legs and, dropping his chin on his paws, looked up at Steppin anxiously. Surely Steppin could not mean that. Hadn't he, Pedigree, been praised many a time for his prowess as a rat-killer? He leaped at Steppin again.

"You get away, you good-for-nothing mutt!" Steppin raised his umbrella threateningly. "You made about enough trouble for one day. Ruined my whole career and almost got me in jail. Keep goin', I tell you!"

Poor Pedigree! Humans were hard to understand sometimes. Here he had tried his best to catch the rat, and now his beloved Steppin was roaring at him as if he had done something wrong. Completely bewildered by Steppin's behavior, he reluctantly slunk away. Steppin took the trembling little rat from his pocket.

"Oh! Look what he's got." Two small boys ran up to Steppin. "Ain't he cute? Lemme see him, will you?"

"Do you want him?" Steppin held the rat toward them.

"Yeah, fine chance!"

"You're foolin', I bet."

The boys backed away suspiciously.

Steppin thrust the rat into the eager hands of the nearest boy. "He's all yours, buddy."

"Oh, thanks. Gee, can you imagine giving him away?"

Steppin spread his hands in a gesture of finality. "You're as welcome as snow in August," he declared fervently as he walked away.

"Hey, what's his name?" the boy called after him.

Steppin stopped and turned to face the boys. "His name is Misery, just plain Misery," he sighed.

CHAPTER 5

Steppin Meets the Theatre Man

"I'm out my dough,
I got no rat,
My job's washed up,
Now just tie that!"

Steppin had settled down on a cement horse block to rest. His feet dangled over the curbstone, and his heels beat out a mournful accompaniment as he chanted his misfortunes.

The rain had ceased, and the avenue was quickly thronged with youngsters enjoying the coolness of the fresh, sun-splashed streets. But Steppin, sitting with his head thrust forward and his chin propped on the crooked handle of the baggy umbrella he held between his knees, had no part in the happy crowd. He looked as forlorn and downcast as if he himself had absorbed all the grey gloom of those three days of drizzling rain.

"Oh, boy, if only I'd had the sense to tie up Pedigree! I might have known he'd get out and come following after me. Now I've got the Elite so down on me I'll never have the nerve to go back. I guess I'm not doing right.

"I'm out my dough
And—thump, thump, thump
My job's—"

Steppin's reiteration of his troubles was rudely interrupted as a big limousine swerved up to the curb, grazing his toes. He jerked up his feet indignantly.

"All I need now is to get my feet run over," he muttered. "Can't he see the no parking sign?"

"Hi, son, will you drop this envelope for me at the box office?" Steppin glanced contemptuously at the handsome man behind the wheel.

"First he cuts my toes off almost, and next he wants me to do him a favor!" Without bothering to answer, Steppin dropped his eyes and stared resolutely at his insulted feet.

"Oh, I beg your pardon, young fellow, I didn't mean to interrupt you."

The pleasant voice of the stranger only added to Steppin's bad humor.

"I'm not doin' anything," he growled. "See?"

The man threw back his head and laughed heartily. "I mean you seem to be communing with Lady Luck."

There was something so warm and friendly about the man's voice that, in spite of himself, Steppin felt his indignation vanishing.

"Mister, I don't know what you're talking about, but I do

know that there's no such thing as Lady Luck or even luck-pieces. If you say there is, I don't want anything to do with it."

The man behind the wheel only smiled more broadly. Then he shot back his cuff and looked at his gleaming wristwatch. "You're a right smart boy. I'll tell you what, you drop this envelope at the box office so I won't have to find a place to park and then suppose we take a little spin in the park, and you tell me what's eating you. Maybe I can do something."

Steppin sprang to his feet. "You can't do a thing, Mister, but I sure would admire to see what one of them showcases feels like when you're riding in it instead of dodging it."

Steppin had not paid any attention to his surroundings when he sat down. Now he realized that he was in front of the old Lafayette Theatre. In the lobby there were huge bill posters advertising a coming attraction.

GALA BENEFIT PERFORMANCE
Featuring Harlem's Most Talented
Sons and Daughters
Starring Bob Williams, Tap Dancer

Steppin's eyes shone as his eyes read the name of the famous dancer. "Boy, I sure would like to see him," he sighed as he hurried up to the box office window and shoved the envelope under the grating.

"A man in a car outside said to give this to you," he explained.

"It's from the boss," he heard the ticket man say to someone.

"The boss—then he must own this theatre." Steppin stared at his new acquaintance with profound respect as he approached the car. It occurred to him that the man's face was vaguely familiar, now that he really looked at him.

"All set?" the stranger asked as Steppin climbed in beside him, and with a gentle purr, the car glided forward.

In the few minutes that it took the high-powered car to reach

Central Park, Steppin found himself talking to this new friend as freely as though he had known him all his life.

"Well, sir," he finished the account of his disastrous afternoon, "after I chased Pedigree home, I got to thinking how awful everything had turned out, and I just sat down on the curb, and there I sat pondering until you came along."

The man had listened sympathetically until Steppin reached the point where Pedigree had made his entrance at the Elite. From then on he began to chuckle louder and louder, until finally he bent over the wheel and roared with laughter.

"Boy, I sure would have liked to see that dancing class when the rat broke loose!"

Steppin, who had been anxiously watching the road, relaxed and laughed too. "Now that I think of it, it was funny to see all those girls shinnying up on the window sills and such," he admitted, "but it wasn't funny then. I thought my time had come for sure. Say, do you own that theatre?" Steppin changed the subject abruptly. "When I handed over the envelope, the man said it was from the boss."

"Well, I don't exactly own it," the man grinned, "but they do know me pretty well around there."

"The reason I asked," Steppin explained, "is I thought if you owned a theatre, you'd know a lot about dancers, and maybe you could tell me the name of another school I could try."

"Well, I do know quite a few hoofers," the man admitted. "And I wouldn't be surprised if I know just the school for you."

"Is it very—I mean, does it cost much?" Steppin asked anxiously.

"Not very much. In fact, if I asked him to, I think the teacher would take you and let you pay a little at a time. Then if you really had something, he might let you work out your tuition by cleaning the studio, running errands, and things like that."

Steppin's eyes sparkled. He was just going to ask how long it usually took before he could become a dancer when the car stopped.

"Well, here we are, right back where we started from," the man said cheerily. And sure enough, they were again parked at the curb in front of the theatre. Steppin looked up at the building.

"Lafayette Theatre," he said softly. "Maybe even Bob Williams stands here sometimes, thinking about dreams like I was, only I don't know what he could wish for—he's got just about everything already."

"Don't you believe it," the man assured him. "As a matter of fact, I've heard tell he comes here often—remembering and dreaming."

"You don't say!" Steppin exclaimed. "I wonder what he could want that he hasn't got. He don't have to go to school, he's bound to have all the money he needs, and, on top of that, he's the best tap dancer in the whole wide world."

"Oh, he is, is he?" laughed the man. "I wonder whoever told you that."

"Told me!" exclaimed Steppin. "Why, Mister, everybody just knows that's the truth."

"You don't say!"

Something about the way the man was grinning made Steppin feel he was being laughed at.

"Oh, you're just fooling with me," he grinned back. "You know Bob Williams is the world's greatest tap dancer just as well as anyone."

"Well, I'm willing to admit I've never seen anyone I thought was better," the man conceded. "But now, about that school I mentioned a while back."

Steppin waited eagerly while his new friend took a small notebook from his inside coat pocket and, after scribbling a few lines, tore out a page.

"Suppose you take this to the address I've written here at round about nine o'clock tomorrow morning, Steppin, and see what happens."

Steppin buttoned the note in his shirt pocket before he climbed out of the car.

"I hardly know how to begin to thank you," he stammered. The stranger leaned over and gave Steppin a friendly clap on the shoulder.

"Oh, that's all right, sonny; I'm always glad to do a good turn for anyone in the profession."

"In the profession." Steppin said the words over softly as the limousine whirred off. "Gosh, that makes me feel like I'm on the stage already." And then, with a sudden flash he thought, "Maybe he is in the profession, too. Maybe I've been riding around with a sure enough professional all morning and didn't even know it."

Then with a pang of regret, he realized that he hadn't even found out his benefactor's name!

Just then he heard a gentle "wuff" behind him. Pedigree, who had been lurking about ever since his stern dismissal, had decided it was time to resume friendly relationships. When Steppin called his name, Pedigree jumped into his arms, quivering with joy.

Steppin rubbed his cheek against the dog's wiry ruff.

"Good old puppy," he said affectionately. "Sometimes you're not very bright, but don't you worry about it."

"You know what, Pedigree," Steppin continued as the two set off for home. "They say it's a sin and a shame to wish your life away, but I'd give up a month of mine if I could wish nine o'clock tomorrow morning here right now."

CHAPTER 6

The Kirby
Professional Class

Bright and early the next morning, Steppin was hurrying along a dingy Harlem side street lined on each side with a solid row of shabby brownstone houses. He stopped before one of them and checked the number with the address on the precious slip of paper that the Theatre Man had given him. Then for the hundredth time, he read the message on the slip.

"Dear Dad. This is Steppin. Try him out as a K.P." There was no name signed except a long, sprawling letter B.

Steppin shook his head and sighed heavily. "No matter how many times you read it, the note don't seem to make sense," he thought. He put the slip of paper back in his shirt pocket and turned his attention to the house. In the corner of the window on the parlor floor, he saw a small placard which read "Kirby Professional Class."

"That's it, all right," he decided. He ran up the cement steps to the high stoop and into the hallway. The double doors of the classroom were open. Coming in out of the bright sunshine, the bare, high-ceilinged room seemed dark and gloomy to Steppin, peering into it. A boy of about his own age was sweeping the floor and whistling cheerfully. When he saw Steppin, he stopped whistling and grinned at him.

"Hi," he greeted Steppin briskly.

"Hi," Steppin replied.

"New kid, huh?" the boy asked.

Steppin nodded.

"K.P. or star boarder?"

For a minute Steppin didn't know what to say. Then he remembered the note. "I'm a K.P., whatever that is," he told the boy.

"You'll find out what a K.P. is soon enough," the boy chuckled. "I'm a K.P. myself. That's why I have to come early and police the place—sweep and dust and like that before class."

"Then a K.P. is a kid who works for his lessons?" Steppin asked.

"That's the idea," the boy nodded. "We call it doing Kitchen Police—K.P. for short. You can just rest yourself somewhere and watch me," he offered hospitably. "Then you'll know what has to be done. I reckon you'll be taking my place before long. I got to go and have an operation in the hospital," he confided proudly.

"Gee, that's tough!" Steppin sympathized.

"Oh, it's nothing much," the boy explained modestly. "I just got to have my tonsils and adenoids cut out."

"I guess that isn't so much," Steppin agreed. "I had mine out once when I was little, and I don't even remember about it."

"I've got a very bad case though," the boy assured Steppin. "When I sleep, I snore so loud you can hear me for blocks. I'll most likely choke to death if I don't get them cut out."

Steppin looked impressed. "Golly!" he exclaimed.

The boy seemed gratified at Steppin's concern. "Well, I've got to get my work done before Dad comes down." He picked up the broom and started sweeping.

"Who is Dad?" Steppin inquired.

The K.P. stopped short and stared at Steppin with amazement.

"Don't you know who Dad Kirby is?" he asked.
Steppin shook his head. "I guess that's tore out of my book," he said with a grin.

"Say, how come you're here if you never heard about Dad Kirby?"

Steppin felt embarrassed at his ignorance. "Why—I—well, you see a friend of mine recommended the school to me," he explained.

"Well, if you're fixin' to hang around here, you'd better find out who Dad is," the boy warned Steppin. "Why, Dad *runs* this place, and when I say *runs,* I mean *runs.* Just seeing him casual, you might get the idea that he was soft-going, maybe. And he is a right man, too, so long as no one tries to handle him with rough kid gloves. But if anyone starts messin' around with Dad—boy, oh boy—can he hand out thunder and lightnin'!"

Just then a sound of slow footsteps and the tap-tap of a crutch could be heard from the hall stairs.

"That's Dad now," hissed the boy.

Steppin watched curiously as the sound of the slow footsteps came closer, and Dad Kirby, walking with a crutch, appeared in the doorway. He was little and shabby and rather oldish, Steppin noticed. At least his grey hair and eyebrows, which looked snow-white against his brown skin, made him seem old. His face was young-looking, however, and in spite of his lameness he carried himself very straight, almost like a soldier, Steppin thought.

"Morning, Dad," the K.P. greeted him politely.

"Good morning, Roddy. It appears like it's taking you a long time to get the place policed," he said mildly.

"I'm just about done. I was talking to the new boy," Roddy apologized, nodding his head towards Steppin.

Steppin approached Dad and silently handed him the note. Dad read it and looked Steppin over appraisingly. Then he smiled and shook his hand.

"Pleased to meet you, Steppin. I'm always glad to give any friend of the boss a chance," he said pleasantly.

Steppin was just about to explain that he really didn't know much about the "boss" when there was a sudden uproar in the hall, and several young boys barged noisily into the room. At the same time, a shrill, angry voice began to screech, "Go home, go home, your mother wants you."

Steppin turned in the direction of the voice and saw a large parrot in a cage which Roddy had just uncovered.

More boys came trooping in, and Steppin thought he had never seen a stranger assortment of outfits than these boys were wearing. Some were attired only in faded, stretched-out cotton bathing suits. Some wore nothing but overalls, while others wore shabby, patched trousers and no blouses.

"They all look as if they were dressed up for a Thanksgiving rag-a-muffin parade," thought Steppin.

The boys shouted noisy greetings to Dad and to each other. Several of them began practicing tap steps on the hardwood floor. The parrot ruffled her bright feathers and clawed at the bars of the cage. "Go home, line up, don't mush it, pipe down, Minnie—front two three," she screeched.

"It's more like a crazy house than a dance school," thought Steppin as, alone and self-conscious, he stood watching them. "I wonder when the teacher is coming."

In the meantime, Dad Kirby had settled himself in an armchair in one corner of the room and, apparently oblivious to the din around him, was quietly puffing away on a corn cob pipe.

When a clock on the wall struck nine, he put his pipe down and stood up.

"All right, kids, line up for limbering and stretching. Make it snappy! Roddy, you show Steppin the ropes."

There was a moment of scuffling confusion as the fifteen boys took their places at the long bars on either side of the room. With a sinking heart, Steppin took a place behind Roddy.

"More exercise," he thought. "Just like that old Elite."

Dad hobbled to the middle of the room, and leaning heavily on his crutch, he wound up an old-fashioned phonograph and set the needle on the disc.

"Pipe down, Minnie," he scolded the parrot who was screeching, "Line up, let's go," over and over. "Pipe down, Minnie," the parrot echoed.

After a few raucous turns, the phonograph grated out a noisy rendition of "The Stars and Stripes Forever." Dad sat down on a stool and faced the class.

"High kicks," he commanded. "All set? Let's go! Kick to the front, to the side, and straight back," he shouted above the blatant music as he counted the steps. Whenever he interrupted himself to correct a pupil or to chide Minnie, he kept the time by thumping his crutch on the floor.

"Front—two, three; side—two, three; back—two, three; about face."

With the precision of soldiers, the boys turned and faced the great framed full-length mirror at the opposite side of the room.

"Repeat with the left leg! Front—two, three; side—two, three; Steppin, don't bend your knees, kick higher, aim for the moon."

Relentlessly, Dad kept on counting and thumping until the last note of the march sounded. Then he rewound the machine and put on a new record.

"Back bends," he announced briefly.

The boys faced the wall and held onto the bar with both hands.

"Bend back on three counts and come up on three counts."

Steppin did his best to follow, but his heart was not in it. Besides, he was getting out of breath. "Oh, golly!" he sighed. "Why can't I ever find a real dance teacher that teaches dancing!"

"Bend, Steppin, bend—you won't break. Back and up, back and up!"

The relentless voice of Dad boomed on and on, stopping only while he wound the phonograph and changed the records. Finally, just as Steppin decided he was about to drop dead, Dad shouted, "Rest," and the music stopped.

"Take a three-minute recess and then get set for floor work." Dad hobbled back to his armchair and settled down for a break.

At the welcome announcement, the line of perspiring, panting boys broke. Some of them made a beeline for the water cooler while others sat or lay on the floor. A few of the more energetic remained at the bar practicing splits. Steppin jerked a grimy handkerchief from his hip pocket and sopped up the beads of sweat which made his face glisten like polished bronze. Then he quietly slipped out through the front door and flopped down on one of the grim stone lions which guarded the steps of the old brownstone house. Steppin didn't look as though he had at last realized his ambition to join a professional tap dancers' class. He was frowning so hard that his heavy eyebrows met over his nose, and his lower lip was thrust forward sulkily.

"Kick to the front, kick to the side, kick to the back," he muttered angrily. "Bend fo'wards and back, do this and do that, until I'm so tired I can't hardly budge, to say nothing of dance. What a way to learn to be a professional. I been here a whole hour almost, and I haven't learned a dance yet. Why can't they teach you dances instead of keeping you hung on a railing doing those fool limberings and stretchings they're all so crazy about. 'The Kirby Professional Class'!" Steppin kicked the lion's flank contemptuously. "It sure looks professional, with that crazy parrot screeching and the kids wearing any old clothes, even bathing suits, and a poor old lame man for a teacher!"

The sound of the wheezy old phonograph grinding out a fox trot made Steppin jump to his feet. Recess was over. Reluctantly he went back to the classroom. The boys were lined up in rows in the center of the room where Dad was explaining a step to them. Roddy was standing beside Dad to demonstrate the step. "On the count of one, bend your left knee and lunge forward—reach forward with your left arm, and let your right arm and right leg slide straight out behind. Reverse on count two. Try it without music."

"One and two and one and two," Dad counted out, as the boys tried the step with varying success.

"Lunge and slide and lunge and slide—don't forget to reach with the opposite arm. Slide all the way back. Finish each count before you start the next. Keep your steps neat—don't mush it— lunge and slide and one and two.

Steppin had never tried a step like this before. He found that just keeping his balance was about all that he could manage.

Twice he had to let his forward arm touch the floor to keep from falling flat on his face. To his great relief, if Dad noticed, he made no comment.

After the boys had practiced the step without music until they were breathless, Dad called them to attention.

"Well, you seem to have a vague idea of how the step goes," he granted them grudgingly. "Now try and remember that you are supposed to keep together instead of every man for himself. Take it to music."

Dad opened the upright piano, and then he sat down on the bench and struck a chord.

"Now all together. Keep right on going until I tell you to stop. Don't mush it!"

The piano sounded like a full band after that rasping old canned music. Steppin felt for the first time that morning a desire to dance. Although he had never tried anything so complicated as this, he was determined to do it well. He watched

Roddy, who was still up in front as monitor, and tried to do the step exactly right.

"Maybe if I show him I'm good, he'll put me on learning dance routines instead of wasting my time on these steps and exercises," he thought hopefully.

"Lunge and slide and lunge and slide. One and two and one and two," Dad counted as his long black fingers skillfully struck chords. Over and over the count went on.

Before he called a halt, Steppin was so tired that he was barely going through the motions of the step. The crouching position cramped his legs, and his knees felt first hot and painful and later so numb that they hardly supported him. Just when he felt that he couldn't possibly last a second longer, Dad stopped playing and called, "Time out!"

The entire class collapsed on the floor. Steppin heard sighs of relief on every side. Even the monitor was breathing heavily.

"Now while you are resting, I'll explain the break." And Dad plunged into a careful description of the next step. Presently, Roddy went through it under Dad's direction, and before Steppin, or, in fact, any of them had had time to half-recover from their previous work, Dad was ready to begin. After they had practiced the new step a few times, Dad sat down at the piano and gave them the routine for combining the steps.

"Do the lunge and slide for twelve counts," he directed, "then when I give you the break, twist on one foot without straightening up, pull yourself up after the twist, then six straight steps, and finish with twelve triple taps."

Steppin's head swam. It seemed to him that the steps as Dad outlined them were utterly impossible for any human being to perform. However, he doggedly determined to make an attempt at it.

"Lunge and slide and lunge and slide." Steppin tried his best to keep up with Dad's count, although the hot pain in his knees was almost more than he could bear. He managed to keep

going, and when Dad struck the chord for the break he tried the
quick, crouching twist. With an almost superhuman effort to
keep from falling over backwards, he jerked himself up, only to
fall flat on his face. As he scrambled to his feet, he felt a warm
sticky, trickle of blood from his bruised nose, and he heard
someone snicker. There was a thundering chord from the piano,
and as he nursed his nose in his handkerchief, Steppin heard
Dad's voice roar out, "That will do, Lester!" There was dead
silence in the room. After a few seconds Dad spoke again.

"Since when have you got yourself so perfected you have any
call to laugh at someone else?" Dad scowled at the completely
paralyzed Lester, and his white teeth flashed as he thundered
reproof. Even in his misery, Steppin's eyes were riveted on the
lowering cloud of Dad's face and the flashing of white teeth. "He
sure can hand out thunder and lightnin'." Now he knew what
Roddy meant.

"And as far as that goes," Dad snapped, "If ham dancing was
any cause for laughing, I'd have laughed myself to death long ago."

"Steppin," Dad turned and spoke kindly, "I think you've had
enough for today, and for a beginner you did right smart to
keep up in this class as long as you did. All you need is more
ground work. Suppose you come to beginners' class tomorrow.
That's at eleven. You'll get more basic stuff—balancing, limbering, and stretching. That's what you need."

Steppin nodded dully. He couldn't trust himself to speak.
With his nose buried in his handkerchief, he walked blindly out
of the room. He paused on the step and, after an anxious glance
around, gave his eyes as well as his nose a dab with his handkerchief. Then he walked slowly down the steps and aimlessly
along the blistering-hot street. Without thinking much of where
he was going, he wandered into the park, and after wetting his
handkerchief and taking a long drink at the geyser fountain,
he found a secluded shady spot and threw himself facedown
on the grass. He pressed the cold, wet handkerchief against his

throbbing nose and swallowed hard. The pain in his nose was nothing to the pain of his hurt feelings. To have made a spectacle of himself by falling, and then to have Dad add to his embarrassment by making such a scene about it, was bad enough. But the crowning blow to his pride was to be told in front of the whole class that he was only good enough for a beginners' class.

"More limberings and stretchings, my eye!" he muttered indignantly. "Who does he think I am, anyway?"

The more Steppin thought about Dad's parting remark, the angrier he became. Anger helped to restore his self-respect so that after a while, his head began to clear a little.

"I got to ponder on this," he muttered. "The whole trouble," he finally concluded, "is that I never got a chance to explain myself. Maybe if I could make Dad see that I'm just interested in learning routines and don't want to waste my time on exercises and doing the same steps over and over, he could fix me up. Or if he don't want to take me on those terms, maybe he knows someone else that would."

"The class ought to be over, about," he thought. "If I go back now, I might get a chance to speak to him right off."

Steppin felt better now that he had made up his mind what to do. After he had refreshed himself by plunging his swollen face into the cool geyser of the drinking fountain, he felt almost cheerful. He was a little uneasy as to how Dad would take his proposal.

"If I keep polite and respectful and just explain what I want, it shouldn't cause any thunder and lightnin'," he reassured himself.

As Steppin turned into the side street, he saw a sight that filled him with longing. The fire hydrant was open, and a great column of water roared and splashed across the street. Dozens of boys and girls, some in bathing suits and some in disreputable old garments, were shrieking and frolicking under the powerful spray. More and more children were pouring out of the houses to take advantage of the treat before one of the firemen from the local station would return to shut off the flow. Every day during the hot weather, the city provided this cooling shower for children cooped up in the city streets.

"Boy, I sure would like to get under that water about now," Steppin sighed. "They most likely have our hydrant on too, and I'll miss out all around."

When Steppin reluctantly tore himself away from the tempting scene and climbed the steps to the Kirby Professional Class, he saw a dozen or more pairs of boys' shoes heaped together on the stoop. So that was why the boys wore such outrageous-looking clothes! Every boy in the class but Steppin was cooling off under the street shower.

The door to the classroom was closed. "Come in," Steppin heard Dad's voice respond as he knocked. When he tried the door, he found it was locked.

"Come in!" Dad's voice sounded impatient.

"I can't open the door," Steppin exclaimed.

"Well, go home then." For a moment Steppin was so surprised that he couldn't speak. Then suddenly he realized that it was Minnie the parrot and not Dad to whom he was talking. He burst out laughing.

"Ha, ha, ha!" the voice mimicked. "Go home, your mother wants you—pipe down, Minnie! Ha, ha, ha!"

The parrot was making such a din and Steppin himself was laughing so hard that he had not heard the quick, light footsteps of someone running down from the second floor.

"Hello there!" a cheerful voice called out almost in his ear. Steppin turned with a start and found himself face to face with the Theatre Man.

"Well, how do you like Dad's joint?" The man's smiling brown eyes took in Steppin's swollen nose and forlorn appearance, but he made no mention of it.

Steppin's surprise and pleasure at meeting his new friend were quickly followed by dismay. It was going to be hard to

explain his disappointment in the school after the man had
taken so much trouble to help him.

"Dad's all right, only—" Steppin stopped and looked down at
his feet.

"Only what?" The man took a key from his pocket and
opened the door. "What's the trouble?" he continued as Steppin
hesitated. "Is Dad making you work too hard?"

"No, it ain't that; I don't mind work," Steppin assured him.

"Well, what's biting you then?"

Steppin raised his head and took a long breath. "Well, to tell
you the truth, Mister, this isn't just the kind of school I had in
mind—all these exercises and such. I mean, you see, I know
how to dance already, and all I want is someone to teach me
some good routines so I can get a job."

As Steppin blurted out his explanation, he watched the face
of the Theatre Man anxiously. The man looked surprised at first,
Steppin thought, but after that he listened quietly, and for the
life of him Steppin couldn't decide how he was taking it. "Oh,
I see," was all he said when Steppin had finished. For a minute
the Theatre Man stood scratching his chin and looking gravely
down at Steppin. Then he suddenly pushed open the door of the
classroom.

"Well, maybe you are right," he said pleasantly. "Come on in
and show me what you can do."

"Do you mean you want me to dance right now?" Steppin
asked.

"Sure, I do." The man dropped the cover over the bird cage
to silence Minnie, who was still shrieking at them. Then he sat
down at the piano and began playing.

"All right, cut loose," he commanded. Feeling very foolish,
but not knowing what else to do, Steppin caught step with the
music and started to dance.

"Brush, brush and hop, and brush, brush and hop," he
counted out the beats, as he went through the only routine he

knew. Tired as he was, he was trying to do his best. He even managed to do a fairly good cartwheel and split for the finish. Then he stood up and waited silently for the verdict.

There had been a strange smile on the man's face as he watched Steppin. Now, still smiling, he shook his head.

"Not bad for a beginner," he said. Then, taking pity on Steppin's speechless misery, he stopped smiling.

"Steppin, have you ever seen any first-class tap dancing, big Broadway stuff I mean, and not this street jiggling you call dancing? Because if you haven't," he continued before Steppin could answer, "you're sure going to before you're a day older. In other words, I'm going to give you a pass to see the show at the Lafayette Theatre tonight."

"Do you mean a pass to see Bob Williams at your theatre?" The misery in Steppin's face turned to incredulous amazement. "That's exactly what I had in mind," the Theatre Man declared. He produced his little notebook and started to write in it. "Have you some buddy you'd like to take along?" he asked. Steppin was almost stuttering with excitement. "If it's not too much trouble, I'd admire to take my mother and sister—maybe you could write it so they would admit me and family," he suggested.

The Theatre Man smilingly wrote, "Admit Steppin and Family" and signed it with the same sprawling letter B that he had written on the note to Dad.

"Now cut along home," he ordered when Steppin tried to thank him.

Clutching the precious paper, Steppin raced down the steps and started on a dead run for home. He forgot that he was tired and that the day was hot. For the first time in his life, he was going to see a real show, and Bob Williams, the greatest tap dancer on earth, was in it!

CHAPTER 7

Steppin and Family Attend a Gala Performance

Steppin felt like a conquering hero as he raced through the dark hallway to the kitchen. He could hardly wait to tell his mother and Mary Ellis about the wonderful surprise he had for them. "Mom, Mom!" he called impatiently as he pounded on the door.

Mary Ellis opened it, and when she saw Steppin, she stared at him as if he were a stranger. Her eyes opened so wide that they showed white.

"Oh!" she gasped.

Steppin rushed past her to his mother, who was sitting by the stove shelling peas.

"Mom, guess what happened—" He stopped abruptly and stared at his mother, who was staring back at him exactly as Mary Ellis had done.

"*Stephen Aldrich Stebbins*, what have you been doing?" His mother's tone, as well as the fact that she addressed him by his full name, warned Steppin that she was really angry. But although he racked his brain, vainly, he couldn't figure out what he had done.

"What's the matter?" he asked. His mother pointed towards the mirror over the sink. "Look at your face!" she commanded. "And then ask me what's the matter."

When Steppin saw his reflection in the mirror, it was his turn to gasp. His nose was nearly twice its natural size, and his left eye looked as if he had painted a large circle of purple ink around it.

"Steppin, I don't know what's got possession of you. Sometimes I wonder will I ever raise you to be respectable. If you won't take heed and stop fighting with every rowdy you meet, you're going to walk in trouble all your life long."

"I wasn't fighting, Mom—honest I wasn't," Steppin finally managed to interrupt his mother's scolding.

At this simple statement, his mother and Mary Ellis appeared as shocked as if he had told them he had committed a crime.

"Oh, Steppin, two wrongs never make a right, and lying is worse than fighting," she reproached him.

"Neither do three wrongs make a right." Steppin was getting angry. "Fighting and lying are no worse than accusing people of doing something they didn't do without even giving them a chance to explain." Steppin looked such a picture of outraged innocence that even his mother was impressed.

"Maybe I did overspeak myself," she admitted skeptically. "If you can explain how you got your face that way without fighting, I'll be pleased to listen to you."

"I've been itching to tell you ever since you commenced

worrying at me, Mom," Steppin complained. "Only you wouldn't give me a chance. And when I do make you know I wasn't doing any harm, the both of you will just about hang your heads and weep, I bet!"

Now that he finally had their attention, Steppin took his own good time in telling his story. He was enjoying every minute of it. It was almost worth being accused unjustly to see the contrite look on his mother's face when he explained the innocent reason for his black eye and battered nose. He passed lightly over the Theatre Man's unflattering comments on his dancing.

When he finally got to his big surprise and produced the precious slip of paper, Mary Ellis interrupted his story by jumping up and flinging her arms around his neck.

"Oh, Mom, isn't Steppin wonderful!" she cried. And before he could wriggle loose, she kissed him three hard smacks right on his sore nose.

"Well," Mrs. Stebbins reflected, "I don't know as I'd call him wonderful, but I will say he could be a lot worse than he is. I'm right sorry I misjudged you, Steppin," she added kindly. "And since you thought to remember your sister's pleasure and mine, as well as your own, I won't even mention that it's near about three hours since you were supposed to be home for lunch. Goodness knows," she smiled good-naturedly, "whatever your faults may be, missing your meals is the least of them!"

"I'll fix your lunch, Steppin," Mary Ellis offered sweetly. "I'd just as lief as not. You rest yourself and cool off."

"I don't mind if I do," Steppin sighed.

"Isn't it good I ironed my best dress this morning, Mom? What are you and Steppin going to wear?" Mary Ellis kept up a constant happy chatter as she tripped back and forth with food for Steppin.

"Steppin will wear his best suit, and I'll wear my blue silk print, of course," Mrs. Stebbins decided. "I think we will get everything ready and laid out beforehand. Then we'll have an early supper, and we will have time for a bath apiece before we dress."

It was fun preparing for the marvelous evening ahead. Mary Ellis was just as excited as Steppin, and even Mrs. Stebbins seemed shaken out of her usual quiet dignity as they hustled about preparing their clothes. Mary Ellis pressed Steppin's long pants and washed and ironed the lace collar of her mother's dress. Then she went over her pink organdy, pressing out imaginary wrinkles, and ironed her best wide, pink moire hair ribbons. Mrs. Stebbins attended to last-minute darning and mending and sewing on of buttons, while Steppin gave their shoes what he called "a genuine ten-cent shine." By five o'clock there was a complete outfit on each of their beds, even to a clean handkerchief apiece.

They made quick work of the cold supper Mary Ellis prepared. For once, even Steppin's appetite failed him. Steppin and Mary Ellis were so afraid they might be late that they insisted upon getting ready the minute they had washed and dried the supper dishes. As a result, all three were dressed and ready to leave a good two hours before it was time for the show to begin.

"Do you think it would look all right if I went without a hat, Mom?" Mary Ellis asked anxiously. "I hate to squash my hair ribbons."

"I'm sure it would," Mrs. Stebbins assured her. Mary Ellis took a final admiring look at her reflection in the mirror. Then she turned her attention to her mother and brother. "You look lovely, Mom, and so does Steppin," she began, but being a very truthful little girl, Mary Ellis stopped herself just in time, for of course Steppin's eye detracted considerably from his appearance.

"My looks have got me bothered, too," Steppin sighed. "But I just *couldn't* not go."

"Never mind, Steppin," Mrs. Stebbins comforted him. "After all, you are going to see and not to be seen. Probably no one will take much heed of you, anyway."

"Oh, Steppin, I've got an idea—wait!" Mary Ellis ran into The Wreck of the Hesperus and returned with a pair of thick, horn-rimmed play spectacles that she had once worn in the role of Mother Hubbard in a school play.

"Put them on, Steppin." Mary Ellis jumped up and down and clapped her hands as Steppin's eyes peered out at them through the wide, dark rims. "Didn't I tell you? You can hardly notice the black and blue at all."

"It certainly makes him less conspicuous," his mother agreed. And Steppin, after the first shock at seeing his altered appearance, decided it was a great improvement.

Mary Ellis carefully pinned in the buttonhole of his lapel two white sweet peas which she had picked from her garden and stood back to study the effect.

"I think he looks right distinguished," she declared. "With long pants and glasses, he looks so grown up you'd almost take him for a family man."

Steppin, who had been anxiously watching the clock, declared it was time to start for the theatre.

Just as they were ready to leave, Mrs. Stebbins went to her room. She came back looking very mysterious, carrying in her hand a small old-fashioned carved box.

"Children, I have a little surprise for you," she announced. "I've been saving these for your graduation presents when you finished high school. But I've been thinking it over, and I don't know as you'll ever have a better occasion to wear them."

She opened the box and lifted out a heavy gold watch and chain and an old-fashioned gold locket with its chain. "Oh, Mom!" Steppin and Mary Ellis cried out.

"This was your father's watch, so it rightly belongs to you," his mother told Steppin as she handed it to him.

"And Mary Ellis, this was your father's wedding present to me. It has the both of our wedding pictures in it."

"It's so beautiful." Mary Ellis' voice was trembling and her eyes sparkled. "And look, it's got an opal setting just like my birthday ring," she exclaimed, putting her little brown ring finger and the locket side by side.

"That's because the opal is my birthstone, too," Mrs. Stebbins smiled as she hung the chain around her daughter's neck.

"After tonight I wonder will I ever get excited anymore," Steppin declared, putting the watch in his vest pocket and carefully arranging the chain across his front. "I bet even when Christmas morning comes, I won't hardly bother to wake up!"

Mrs. Stebbins shook her head, smiling skeptically. "I wish I could depend on that, but I'm afraid, to my sad disappointment, that when the day comes you'll be tearing around the house before dawn as always," she prophesied.

It was only a few blocks from their house to the theatre, and in no time at all they stood before the sparkling electric signs and big posters at the entrance. Steppin, clutching the note, led his family through the brightly lit lobby.

"Tickets, please." The usher gave Steppin a quick, curious glance as he examined the slip of paper. For one awful moment, Steppin feared there might be some mistake and that they would be turned away. He turned hot and cold all at once. "And I don't even know the name of the Theatre Man if he should ask me," he thought miserably.

But the usher bowed and smiled, as though Steppin were his best friend.

"Yes, sir, this way, sir. Just follow me." In his immense relief, Steppin scarcely noticed where the usher was leading them until he stopped before a red-curtained door down a long alley on one side of the theatre. The young man drew aside the curtain, disclosing a closed-in balcony set with four little gilt chairs.

"Box seats!" Steppin was so excited that he half started through the door, but just in time he remembered his manners and stood aside until his mother and Mary Ellis entered.

The usher helped Mrs. Stebbins to a seat, and with the

utmost patience, he waited while Mary Ellis smoothed and shook out her crisp organdy skirt before she would sit down.

"Is there anything I can do for you, sir?" he asked Steppin, handing him three programs.

"I don't think of anything, thank you, sir," Steppin replied, and then with a sudden inspiration he nonchalantly produced his watch. "Could you oblige me with the correct time?" he asked importantly.

The young man glanced at his wrist. "It's exactly one and one-half minutes to eight. I trust you all will enjoy the performance."

"Isn't this the most fun!" Mary Ellis exclaimed with a delighted wriggle as soon as the usher had left. "My goodness, Steppin, your friend *must* be the boss of this place, no fooling."

"You'd think we lived on Sugar Hill or Strivers' Row or something, the way that usher man kowtowed," Steppin chuckled. "I wish I'd had sense enough to find out the Theatre Man's real name."

"That you must do without fail," Mrs. Stebbins said. "For we surely must write him a thank-you letter for his great kindness to us."

Since the show was not scheduled to begin for half an hour, the theatre was almost empty when the Stebbins family arrived. Steppin examined his watch many times, but it was for the pleasure of looking at it, rather than because the time dragged. They read the programs from cover to cover and exclaimed over the exciting list of black singers, dancers, actors, and comedians who were to appear in the performance.

Then they amused themselves by watching the audience arrive. Before long the occasional groups sauntering down the aisles grew to a steady stream of men in tuxedos and swallow-tailed coats and women wearing beautiful gowns and wraps.

As Steppin gazed down at the orchestra pit, he suddenly became aware of the fact that many people were looking up at him and his family. He sat back in consternation. "I wonder if we look all right," he wondered. He began studying his mother and sister as if he had never laid eyes on them before.

Mary Ellis was sitting up very straight, her clasped hands resting on the rail of the box. Except for her shining eyes and glowing golden-toffee brown face, she was as sedate as though she were in church. In her pretty pink dress, with two big perky ribbon bows on her hair, she looked like a big brown-and-rose butterfly. Steppin had often heard people say that she was a very pretty little girl.

And no lady could look any nicer than his mother, with her kind, quiet face above her lace collar and her spotless-white gloved hands resting in the lap of her nice blue-and-white silk dress.

Nearly every seat was taken now, and even the boxes were filling.

"Oh, look, Steppin," Mary Ellis whispered, staring at two women sitting just above their box. "Did you ever see such beautiful ladies? You'd think they had stepped right out of the movies."

Steppin regarded the bare brown backs and arms of the two women with disapproval. "You'd think, with all that jewelry, they could afford to buy a whole dress instead of hardly enough to cover them," he sniffed.

Mary Ellis was busy deciding which of the ladies she would choose to be if she could. The lady in red chiffon with the big red velvet flower in her glistening black hair was beautiful, but at the same time the lady in the shining gold-colored dress with a Spanish comb in her hair, solid with many colored stones, was beautiful too. Mary Ellis was still trying to make up her mind when a little bell rang, the house lights lowered, and the first curtain parted.

Behind the curtained stage, an orchestra began to play softly. Steppin and Mary Ellis recognized the music as the theme song of the world-famous band billed on the program. Then, when the asbestos curtain rolled up, they joined in the burst of applause that swept over the theatre.

The entire band was on the stage. As they played, changing colored lights—purple, green, and yellow—shone and shifted over their gorgeous bright blue-and-gold uniforms. The gleaming brass and silver of their instruments flashed and twinkled against a backdrop of blue velvet bearing the monogram of the band leader in silver letters ten feet high.

While Steppin and Mary Ellis clutched hands, breathless before the spectacle, the music suddenly stopped. The stage lights flashed on, and the master of ceremonies walked out from the wings to a microphone. After a few words of greeting, he introduced the band leader, who stepped forward and took a bow.

There was another thundering roar of applause from the audience. The leader bowed and smiled and made a sign to the orchestra. The men rose and bowed too. When the clapping and cheering died away, the leader turned and raised his baton.

A blare of shrill, exciting sound burst from the gleaming instruments. Steppin had never heard such music. It seemed, he thought, to get right inside of you and make you go with it. His feet began tapping in time with the music. Mary Ellis was softly clapping her hands. A wave of excitement ran through the theatre. Hands were clapping and feet tapping, people began to sway and nod their heads, and voices burst out in snatches of the band's tunes.

And as if a band like that wasn't entertainment enough to last a lifetime, the master of ceremonies began calling out one famous artist after another to perform for them.

There was a comedian, who did and said such funny things that your stomach got all tied up from laughing. Then a beautiful woman singer in gleaming white satin with a rhinestone crown on her head was introduced. She came to the microphone and sang blues songs in a sweet, husky voice that made you feel sad but happy too. Another comedian cracked

jokes with the band leader and the audience and finally got
into a make-believe quarrel with a man sitting right behind
the Stebbins' box. For a moment, Mary Ellis and Steppin were
fooled into thinking it was a real quarrel, and then they had to
laugh at themselves.

Once more the band burst into swinging music, ending with
a final, thrilling roll of drums and crash of brass cymbals. The
minute the house lights came on, Steppin seized his program
and ran his finger down to the word "Intermission."

"He's next," he exclaimed. "See," he pointed out to Mary Ellis.
"Bob Williams—he's right after the intermission."

To their surprise, the party in the box behind them had left.
Then they noticed that all over the house, people were leaving
their seats and strolling toward the lobby.

"They act like they've been took down crazy," Steppin
marveled. "I wouldn't budge out of here, and maybe not get
back in time, for anything less than a three-alarm fire."

The ten-minute intermission dragged so slowly that Steppin
had to put his watch to his ear to convince himself that it hadn't
stopped. When the lights did at last go out and the curtain rose,
the murmur of many voices stopped abruptly. You could almost
hear the excited hush that fell over the house. Steppin strained
forward, propped his chin on the rail, and waited impatiently
while the master of ceremonies made his little speech.

"And now, ladies and gentlemen," he finally concluded, "I
take great pride in introducing the world's greatest tap dancer.
Allow me to present for your pleasure the one and only Bob
Williams!"

As Harlem's prime favorite stepped from the wings into
the spotlight, the audience broke out into a deafening roar of
welcome. They clapped and stamped their feet and yelled and
whistled, until the house shook.

Steppin clapped and yelled at the top of his lungs until he
got his first good look at the famous dancer. Then, after an

astonished gasp, he gave Mary Ellis a jab in the ribs that nearly knocked her off her chair.

"It's him, it's him," he yelled in her ear.

"Him, who?" Mary Ellis shouted back as soon as she got her breath.

"It's the Theatre Man," Steppin cried.

"Where?" asked Mary Ellis.

"On the stage—he is Bob Williams!"

Just then the Theatre Man raised his hand, and the house became so quiet that you could have heard a pin drop. As easily and chattily as though he were at home in his own parlor, the dancer began talking to the audience. He told them funny stories about other members of the cast. You could tell by the things he said that he was a good friend to all of them and that he admired their work. His own pianist was on the stage, and now Bob brought him into the conversation, too.

"How about a little tune about now, Dandry?" he asked. When the pianist began playing, Bob just stood there listening and nodding his head to show how much he was enjoying his friend's music.

"Dandry sure can make a piano talk," he remarked after he had joined in the applause which greeted the pianist's work.

Steppin was getting worried for fear Bob Williams might not be going to dance after all, when finally the dancer asked:

"Well, what are we waiting for?" Everybody laughed and began shouting, "Do your stuff, Bob, do your stuff."

Bob raised his derby and set it back on his head at a jaunty angle. He grinned at his pianist.

"All right, Dandry, let's go to town." Bob started saunter- ing across the stage with a quick, light step, swinging his cane. Then, still just sauntering along, his feet began to tap.

"To look at him, anyone would think he wasn't dancing at all," Steppin thought. He just seemed to be strolling along in time to the music. But as he strolled, his feet were beating out taps as fast and sharp as the pip-pip of a machine gun. Steppin had never dreamed that tap dancing could be like this. Not once did Bob drop into any of the grotesque postures or strenuous gymnastics that Steppin used. Bob's dance was like a duet in which Dandry carried the accompaniment and Bob played the melody with his feet.

"How ever does he do it?" Steppin leaned so far over the railing that his mother reached out and clutched his coattail. But, for the life of him, Steppin couldn't follow the lightning pattern of Bob's tapping feet.

"When I think I had the brass to tell *him* I knew how to dance," Steppin sighed. "I'd let myself be took down with the black measles and jumping toothache if I could unsay those words!"

And although part of him went on enjoying every minute of the wonderful performance, another part of his mind went sick with humiliation as he realized how ridiculous his bragging and ham dancing must have seemed to Bob Williams.

Again and again, in response to roars of applause and affectionate shouts from the audience, Harlem's favorite returned to give them the music of his tapping feet and the warmth of his friendly chatter. He was one of them, and they loved him.

When finally the curtain went down, Steppin followed his mother and sister to the street in a daze. He was unusually quiet as they walked home. To his mother's surprise, it was Mary Ellis and not Steppin who insisted that they have sandwiches and cocoa before they went to bed. Mary Ellis chattered away about their wonderful evening while Steppin just sat munching sandwiches and thinking. He scarcely heard what was being said until he heard his name mentioned.

"Do you know what, Mom," Mary Ellis was saying. "I'll bet someday Steppin will be a famous dancer just like Bob Williams. And we'll have so much money, our pockets won't hold. I'll have a piano instead of the old organ, and Steppin will buy you a big car with a chauffeur to carry you around. Won't you, Steppin?"

Steppin swallowed a mouthful of ham and bread.

"Well, I certainly aim to care for you and Mom when I grow up," he agreed. "But I don't expect I'll ever be a great dancer like Bob Williams."

"Oh, yes you will, Steppin, if you try; I just know you will," Mary Ellis insisted.

"I'm sure going to try," Steppin said. "But whether I ever make good is for time to tell. After all, I'm just a beginner. What I need"—Steppin spoke earnestly—"What I chiefly need right now is more basic stuff—like limbering and stretching and such."

CHAPTER 8

Steppin and Harlem's Dread Avengers

"Mom, I aim to be home to help High Pockets with the ash cans around two or thereabouts. Will that be all right?"

"That will do fine, Steppin," Mrs. Stebbins answered. "I'll have High Pockets mop down the stairs and do the halls this morning."

The Stebbins family was at breakfast. Steppin kept his eye on the clock while he crammed a large hunk of buttered hard roll in his mouth and gulped down his cocoa. Then he wiped his mouth and slid out of the Pullman seat of the diner.

"I've got to scram, or the boys will be there before I get the school policed," he announced. "So long!"

As soon as he was gone, Mrs. Stebbins and Mary Ellis smiled broadly at each other.

"I never thought anything could cause Steppin to change like he has," Mary Ellis giggled. "Every night he charges me over and again not to let him oversleep!"

"I declare," said Mrs. Stebbins, "if someone had told me Stephen Aldrich Stebbins would be rising at seven every blessed morning for a whole month of his vacation, I never would have believed it."

"He scarcely takes time to eat," Mary Ellis marveled. "It almost seems like he studies more about his dancing than his stomach."

"It does take up a lot of his time," her mother reflected. "But I don't mind so long as he is so set on it. I've always said if one of you had an honest call you yearned to follow, I'd do everything I could to help you."

Mary Ellis twisted around and hugged her mother. "I know you would, Mom, and I truly think Steppin has a sure 'nuff call to dancing."

Mrs. Stebbins kissed Mary Ellis' shining brown face. "That is as may be," she smiled. "The main thing is he has a big chance, and we must do nothing that might cause him to falter."

Later, when she was washing the dishes, Mary Ellis asked, "Mom, do you reckon maybe I've got a call to play the piano?"

"Well," Mrs. Stebbins considered, "you do play tolerably well, considering you never had any lessons and only an old organ to practice on."

"And about half the keys don't even play," Mary Ellis sighed. "If only we had a real piano! Then, maybe, Steppin would scheme up some way so I could take lessons."

Meanwhile, Steppin had climbed the back fence and was taking a roundabout route to the Kirby Professional Class. For the past two weeks, he had used only the rear entrance to their apartment and shunned all his usual haunts. He did this to avoid meeting Snakey Lewis. Poor Snakey was still trying to persuade Steppin to join Harlem's Dread Avengers so that the gang could use the Stebbins' shed for a clubhouse. Urged on by Butch, the gang leader, Snakey had even taken to hanging around the street entrance, lying in wait for Steppin.

Steppin hoped that if he kept out of sight long enough, the gang would find another clubhouse, and he would be spared the unpleasant task of definitely refusing them the use of the shed. This morning, however, after turning into Lenox Avenue, there was Snakey with his shoeshine box, looking about for early-morning customers. Steppin tried to hurry past, but Snakey was even more persistent than usual.

"Steppin, you'll just haf to hearken to me," he pleaded. "You've caused me to get in an awful jam with Butch and the gang. Butch says I've got to make you join up and let us use the shed, like you promised."

"I don't haf to join up unless I please to," Steppin snorted. "And what's more, it's *my* shed. You can tell Butch it's for me to say who can use it."

"Yes, but Steppin"—Snakey dropped his voice. "I didn't tell you before, but you are in bad too. Butch says if you don't give him an answer right off, he is going to make it hot for you."

"Oh, yeah?" Steppin drawled. "Well, just for that you can tell Butch that I'm not joining, and as for the gang using my shed, the answer is *no!*"

Steppin walked on, leaving Snakey with his mouth gaping open.

"All right for you, Steppin," he shouted. "If you want to mess around with Butch, it's your funeral. You know Butch!"

In one way it was a relief to have the thing settled, but Steppin did feel uneasy as to how Butch would take his message. Butch was older and larger than the rest of his crowd and was a great bully as well.

"Oh, well, I'll dodge him as long as I can, and when the worst comes to the worst, Butch will just about lick me to paper rags," he decided.

The dark classroom seemed refreshingly cool to Steppin as he came in from the sweltering street. Ever since the first day at the school, he had been wearing his bathing suit under his shirt and slacks so he too could take advantage of the street shower. The combination of the intense heat and the scratchy wool suit was almost unbearable.

Although it was a good two hours before the class time, Steppin set about his K.P. duties as if his life depended on it. By a quarter to nine, he had the place swept and dusted and had cleaned Minnie's cage, replenishing her supplies of sunflower seeds and water. He was practicing a tap step when Dad Kirby came limping in from his room on the floor above.

After Dad had wished Steppin "good morning," his sharp eyes glanced around the room.

"You do a right good job of policing the place," he complimented Steppin.

"I aim to," Steppin assured him, "'cause I surely do appreciate getting free dance lessons. I wish I could do more towards paying my way. Especially as you're lettin' me come to beginners' class and advanced class too."

"If working at it will make you a dancer, you're bound to win," Dad chuckled. "I don't have many boys asking for two workouts a morning."

"It's a funny thing, though," Steppin reflected, "but it seems like the more I study at dancing, the worse I get. I used to be tapping around from dawn to dusk, but now just thinking about it gets me all stiff and scared. It's got me bothered. It seems like I just haven't any appetite to dance anymore."

"I've heard tell of that complaint before," said Dad consolingly, "and it's a disease that has to get worse before it gets better. The trouble is that when you were jigging around like you did before, you just thought you were tap dancing. Now you are learning it from the ground up, and at first it's bound to come hard."

"It sure does!" Steppin agreed.

"Steppin," Dad changed the subject abruptly, "there's a new boy joining up with the beginners' outfit this morning. He's a stranger to Harlem as well as to the school. I would mark it a favor if you would look out for him somewhat. Help him get acquainted with some of your friends, and show him around the town, I mean."

"I'll be glad to, sir," Steppin promised.

He felt proud and important as he lined up at the practice bar with the intermediates that morning. He knew everybody in both the boys' classes and laughed and joked with them when they played under the street shower. He knew, too, that there were two classes for girls that met right after lunch. "Only a few weeks ago, I was the new boy," he reflected. He could laugh when he remembered how foolish he had been. He hadn't even known that Bob Williams and Dad were old friends and that Bob often used the classroom to work out his own routines. Now Dad was asking Steppin to show a new boy the ropes. "I must be one of the old boys, sure enough," Steppin thought to himself.

As soon as advanced class was dismissed, Steppin kicked off his shoes, stripped down to his bathing suit, and dashed out to the street shower. But on this day, he cut short his cooling-off period to hurry back to the school.

The new boy had already arrived when Steppin returned. He was about the same age as himself, Steppin noticed, but of a tighter build, with a very dark skin. Steppin liked his pleasant, friendly smile. "He seems like a right enough boy," he reflected.

When Dad had introduced them, the two boys went out to sit on the steps until it was time for the beginners' class. The newcomer watched the boys and girls playing under the shower. Steppin explained the advantage of wearing old clothes or a bathing suit to class as he pulled on his shoes.

"I'm sorry, but I don't recollect what Dad said your name was," he remarked after he had explained the school set-up in detail.

"My name is Pierre Bergeret," the boy answered with a grin.

Steppin looked up in surprise. It was not so much the unusual name as the peculiar accent with which the boy spoke that puzzled him.

"That's a handle I never heard of before," he commented. "Where do you hail from anyway?"

"We are from Haiti." Pierre spoke with the same peculiar accent. "I came to New York only last week."

"Haiti!" Steppin gave such a jerk that he broke his shoestring. "Why, that makes you a foreigner. No wonder you talk so funny."

"I suppose I do," Pierre apologized. "At least everyone here seems to think so. Perhaps it is because I learned French before I learned English. You see, my mother is French."

As the clock in the classroom struck, Steppin knotted his shoestring and stood up. "Let's get inside," he muttered. "Class will be starting in a minute." Pierre looked so bewildered at his new friend's sudden hostility that Steppin felt sorry for him. When the class lined up at the practice bar, he said kindly, "You stand here and follow what I do."

Dad looked over and smiled at him, but Steppin avoided meeting his eyes. "Little does Dad know what he's let me in for," he thought miserably, while he mechanically went through the bar work.

"Out of the whole class of boys, he would have to choose me to make up to a foreigner. What with Butch and the gang down on me anyway, all I need now is for them to catch me messing around with a boy with a handle like Pierre and that talks like he does."

Steppin had reason to be disturbed. It was an unwritten law with the Dread Avengers that any black boy born outside of Harlem was their sworn enemy. As for a foreigner who couldn't even speak plain American, Steppin shuddered at the thought of what would happen if Butch ever heard Pierre talk.

"Steppin, wake up!" Dad's voice broke into his unhappy reflections.

With an effort, Steppin tried to put Butch and the gang out of his thoughts and to concentrate on his work. But in spite of all he could do, his mind kept wandering.

> "Out of one mess
> Right into another
> Trouble loves me
> Like his own twin brother,"

Steppin chanted under his breath as they practiced a new step.

"If I can manage to be friends with him just while we are in the classroom, it won't be so bad," he thought. "But I'd a heap rather Dad asked me to ride down Eighth Avenue on a Bengal tiger than be seen on the street with that kid."

The minute class was over, he made a dash for the door.

"Oh, Steppin," Dad stopped him. "Will you kindly show Pierre the place to get taps put on his shoes? It's right on your way home."

Steppin turned and stared at Dad in dismay. For a moment he could not speak.

"If it's any trouble—" Pierre began politely, then stopped.

Dad's face looked puzzled as he waited for Steppin to answer.

"No trouble at all." Steppin tried to sound convincing as Pierre followed him out of the door.

Somehow, he wasn't at all surprised to see Butch and Snakey waiting at the foot of the street steps. It was like the kind of nightmare in which you know in advance all the terrible things that are going to overtake you. Snakey was looking ready to fight yet apologetic all at once. Anyone could see that he was acting under Butch's orders. Snakey didn't have much sense, but he was as harmless as a kitten. Butch's thick shoulders blocked the way as Steppin and Pierre came down the steps. Steppin thought unhappily, "The rest of the boys will be coming out. If I can only get him away so I won't get licked in front of the whole class!"

"I want to see you, Steppin," Butch announced threateningly.

"I'm in a hurry," Steppin muttered, trying to push past him. "I got an errand to do."

"Oh, yeah?" Butch gave him an ugly smile as he pressed him back. Then, just as he had pictured it, Steppin heard Pierre speaking to him in his precise English with its unmistakable foreign accent.

"If you would give me the address of the shoe place—" he was saying.

For the moment, Butch forgot his original grievance. "Oh boy!" he burst out. "Who dragged this in?"

"You mind your business!" Steppin retorted.

"That's just what I aim to do." Butch glared at him. "And my business is to see that you give me the use of that shed, like you promised Snakey."

Steppin noticed that several boys from the class were loitering about, watching him and Butch. "Let's walk along to the park," he suggested. "We can talk better there."

"Nothing doing," Butch declared. "You've been stalling on me long enough. I'm not taking any more off of you. Come to think of it, I don't know as I even want your shed since you're messing around with mugs like this."

Butch gave Pierre's tie a quick jerk and flipped it up at the boy's face.

"You lay off—" Steppin threatened, then stopped speechless as he saw Pierre's fist shoot out and land on Butch's nose with a resounding thud.

"Why you little—!" But as Butch doubled up, a second quick thrust from Pierre caught him on the chin. With a howl of rage, Butch tore into him. In a minute, there was a ring of motionless boys round the combatants.

Although Butch was half a head taller and twice as heavy as Pierre, no one even thought of interfering in the unequal combat. Pierre had struck first, and it was up to him to take the consequences.

None of them saw Patrolman Burns hurrying across the street toward them. Dad Kirby, who had heard the noise and limped to the door, spied him and motioned for the patrolman to join him.

"Let 'em fight it out, Ted," he wheedled when the officer was within earshot.

Big Ted shook his head dubiously. "Usually I don't pay any attention to their mischief," he said. "But that Butch is the meanest kid in Harlem. Look at the half-pint he picks out to fight!"

"That's Mannie Bergeret's young one," said Dad with a grin. "I've got a notion he can take care of himself."

"You don't tell me!" Officer Burns stepped into the hallway, out of view of any peace-loving citizens passing by. "If that little shaver can lick the biggest hooligan on my beat, I'd sure hate to interfere."

Steppin and the silent ring of observers were getting the surprise of their lives. All of them had figured it would be only a matter of minutes before Pierre would be down and out for good. But although over five minutes had passed, he was still dealing Butch quick, hard punches with deadly accuracy. Butch, on the other hand, was breathing heavily and aiming wild blows that never seemed to reach their goal.

"Look how that little runt dances out of reach—just like a sure enough boxer!" someone exclaimed, and pretty soon they were all cheering Pierre on. Although Butch's left eye was swollen shut and his nose was bleeding, this whole-hearted praise of his rival maddened him even more than the stinging blows from Pierre's quick fists. If he could only get in close enough to grab Pierre, he knew he could trip him and throw him down. An unexpected uppercut from Pierre's left fist caught him with his mouth half open and sank his own teeth into his lower lip. With a roar of pain, Butch rushed in, both arms outstretched and his defense wide open. This was the minute Pierre had been watching for. As Butch bore down on him, he met him with a lightning-fast right-and-left blow to the stomach that bent Butch almost double. He staggered backwards, and his legs seemed to turn to straw as they slowly folded under him.

"Atta boy, beat him to doll's rags," Butch heard the boys yelling, but their voices seemed far off and meaningless as he sat sprawled on the pavement staring vacantly before him. Pierre, the minute Butch hit the ground, had stepped back and stood waiting for him to rise.

"Look at the runt," a voice cried. "He's waiting for the big stiff to get up before he socks him."

"Count him out," another hoarse voice yelled.

"One, two, three," Butch heard the chorus of voices, but the count was half over before its meaning penetrated to him. He shook his head in a vain effort to dispel the haze before his eyes. "Seven, eight," Butch made a half-hearted gesture towards rising and then sank back listlessly. On the count of ten, he was stretched out at full length, his eyes closed, resting as peacefully as a newborn baby.

"Phew!" Big Ted's jolly black face beamed at Dad Kirby. "Bergeret's kid has done more to plug that bully than I could do in a lifetime. I'd have run him in for general delinquency fifty times, if it wasn't that it would have set him up all the more with his gang when he got out."

He ran down the steps and slipped behind a knot of boys who were shaking Butch and fanning him with a piece of cardboard.

"What's going on here?" he growled.

"The cop, cheese it!" A chorus of voices yelled as all but Pierre, Steppin, and Snakey dashed to put a margin of safety between them and the law.

"It was his own fault, Ted, honest it was!" Steppin's voice was tense with earnestness. "Butch started picking on Pierre, and he just got what was coming to him."

"That's right, sir," Snakey chimed in. "I'm a friend to Butch, but I got to admit, he asked for it."

Dad came down the steps carrying a pitcher of water, which he handed to Big Ted. Butch was on his feet now, but he still seemed unaware of what was going on. Big Ted held him at arm's length by his coat collar and gave the pitcher a jerk that shot its contents at Butch's face. The slap of the cold water brought Butch to his senses. Ted tightened his grip as Butch tried to escape. For a minute he stood frowning at Pierre's anxious face. Then he gave him a solemn wink.

"Well, I certainly am amazed," he said; "a great big hulk like you picking on a little boy like Butch Weldon. Why, a boy that would do that would think nothing of pushing little baby ducks in the water. You ought to hang your head in shame. Here, you," he ordered Snakey, "you take our little Butch home to his mama and tell her to put him in a feather bed where he can't come to any harm."

As Big Ted swung down the street, roars of boys' laughter followed him. His chubby black face wore a grin as bright as sunshine. For two years Butch had made his life miserable with his lawless pranks. "But he sure has had to eat dust today," Ted exulted. "And if I know anything about boys' gangs, the Dread Avengers will be looking for a new leader when they get an earful of today's happenings."

Meanwhile, Steppin, feeling that he was in debt to Pierre, had invited him to stop at the Greek's for a soda.

"Honest, Pierre, I didn't aim to let you in for a fight with Butch," he apologized.

"Oh, that's nothing," Pierre assured Steppin. "It wasn't your fault, and I don't mind a fight much anyway."

"Golly, I'll say you don't," Steppin exclaimed. "I sure wish I could handle my mitts like you can!"

"Well," confessed Pierre, "I've probably had more chance than some kids. You see, fighting is my father's business."

Steppin's eyes sparkled.

"You mean your dad's a sure enough prizefighter?"

Pierre nodded.

"Father was lightweight champion when he retired," he confided proudly. "Now he's starting a boxing school here in New York."

"Well, can you tie that!" Steppin regarded Pierre with fervent admiration. "An ex-champ for a father, and you licked the toughest egg in Harlem to boot; and here I was worrying that you would be looked down on just because you were a foreigner."

"Do you think I won't be looked down on now?" Pierre asked anxiously.

"Looked down on! Why, you'll have the gang eating right out of your hands. I don't s'pose there's a kid in twenty blocks that hasn't stood some monkey business or other from Butch Weldon. By laying him low and making him eat humble pie like you did, every one of them will feel you did them a personal favor."

"If that's true, then I'm much obliged to you for giving me the chance to fight him," Pierre laughed, looking much relieved.

"There's only one thing that may go against you," Steppin said earnestly, "and that's your name. It sounds kind of high-toned. So if it's agreeable to you, I'll let out that Pierre is just something your mother calls you, but your everyday handle is 'Pete.'"

"That suits me fine," Pierre assented gratefully.

The boys had finished their sodas and were greedily trying to suck up the last of the tantalizing chocolate froth through the straws when Martie Burns came in.

"Hi," he hailed Steppin.

"Hi, Martie. Meet up with my friend, Pete," Steppin introduced them.

"Say, Steppin. I got three nickels. Sit with me, and I'll treat you all to a pop," Martie offered after shaking hands with Pierre.

"I don't mind if I do," Steppin accepted graciously. "How about you, Pete?"

But Pete, with proper delicacy, wouldn't accept such generosity from a stranger.

"Thanks ever so much, but I must be getting along," he declined politely.

As soon as Pierre spoke, Martie's manner changed from casual friendliness to open hostility.

"Why, that kid's a foreigner," he accused Steppin the minute Pierre had left.

"That's what you think!" Steppin retorted.

"I don't think, I know," Martie insisted. "I've met up with blacks from most every state in the Union, but I never heard an American-born kid talk like that!"

"I suppose you know who Pete's dad is, too," Steppin said sarcastically.

"I don't see any reason why I should," Martie argued. "But I'll bet you dollars to plug nickels he's a foreigner."

"Listen, Martie." Steppin picked his words carefully. "Pete's dad was the world champion lightweight. Not just a small-time boxer, I'm telling you, but the world champion! You can't call a man like that a foreigner. Why, Martie, you know without my telling you that a champion is a champion, and no one gives a hoot even if he was born in Haiti."

Steppin noticed that Martie looked impressed in spite of himself.

"And, what's more," he hurried on, "Pete's father owns a boxing school right here in Harlem. Can you figure what that means to Pete? Why, he gets passes to all the big fights handed out to him like they were last week's streetcar transfers."

"How many can he get?" Martie interrupted eagerly.

"Oh, three or four, I reckon." The eagerness which Martie displayed in regard to passes rather upset Steppin. He decided he had better find out whether there was any truth in his statement before he played it up too heavily. However, he still had not given Martie his best argument in favor of Pierre.

Martie was a member of a rival gang. Although it was organized as the Skull and Cross Bones, a street gang similar to the Dread Avengers, its leaders had been persuaded to reorganize into a Scout Troop. Butch and Harlem's Dread Avengers hated the scouts even more than they had hated the Skull and Cross Bones. It was Butch's proud boast that he had personally licked every scout in the outfit.

"And, listen Martie, that's not all." Steppin interrupted his friend's practical inquiries about the chances of Pete getting passes for both of them and plunged into a glowing account of Pete's battle with Butch. Martie couldn't have been any more attentive if Steppin had been a famous radio announcer giving a ringside account of a championship bout.

"And then, Butch tries to rush Pete, see? And he runs the pit of his stomach plump into a wallop from Pete's right, which wangs out to meet him. Then Pete hands him a hard left, right in the same spot, and Butch folds up and spreads himself out on the pavement like a hunk of butter on a hot griddle."

A smile of deep satisfaction spread over Martie's face as Steppin finished.

"Boy, I sure would have liked to see that," he declared wistfully. "It would be a pleasant change for sure. Every other time I ever heard of a fight with Butch, it finished with me or some other guy sprawled out and Butch sitting on top of us. That Pete must be a right man, for sure."

"Didn't I tell you?" Steppin beamed with triumph. "Listen, Martie, I got five pennies and you still have another nickel. What say we have another pop apiece?"

"Ok," Martie agreed. "Let's drink them to Pete."

"We ought to give him some special nickname like prize fighters have," Steppin urged. "Like Pete the Mauler, or some such name."

"How about 'Pete the Hater'?" Martie asked.

Steppin seemed puzzled. "Why 'Hater'?" he asked.

"Don't you get it!" Martie's voice was slightly patronizing, befitting a genius condescending to the level of a lesser mortal. "What do you call a guy when he comes from New York?"

"A New Yorker—Oh, now I get you." Steppin's scowl vanished as he saw the light. "A guy that comes from Haiti is a Hater."

"Golly, that's great!" And he humbly acknowledged Martie's creative ability.

It was nearer four o'clock than two when Steppin got home. High Pockets was grumbling and sullen because he had to drag out the ash cans by himself. Mrs. Stebbins took Steppin to task for not keeping his word.

Steppin offered a few lame excuses and tried to soothe them with promises to do better. However, he felt that the day's adventures were well worth a little unpleasantness. In the first place, he had practically established Pete as a respected member of the community. And in the second place, his troubles with the Dread Avengers were settled for at least a little while.

CHAPTER 9

Pete Has a Great Idea

The summer days were passing so quickly that Steppin could hardly keep track of them. First it would be Monday, and when he left for the studio, his mother and Mary Ellis would be hanging out the weekly washing. Then it seemed that before he turned around, it would be Friday afternoon and dancing classes would be over for the week. And before he had time to do half the things he planned on Saturday, it would be Sunday with church and Sunday School in the morning and a big dinner in the middle of the afternoon.

It seemed no time at all since the middle of June when school had closed. Now it was nearly the middle of August, and school days were drawing near again.

One scorching hot forenoon, Steppin and Pete were sitting in their bathing suits on the stone steps of the dancing school. Advanced class was just over, and they were waiting for Mr. Harrigan, the fireman, to come and open the street hydrant.

"I'm about fried," Steppin complained. "Unless I feel a sight cooler than I do now, I'm not going to wait for beginners' class."

"I had a good mind not to come at all," Pete confessed. "I guess I don't take dancing as seriously as you do."

"That's because you don't aim to be a professional," Steppin excused him. "You probably lean more to prize fighting like your Dad."

"I don't know for sure," Pete considered. "Sometimes I think I'd like to be a fighter and then again I think I'll keep working at my music and be a pianist or guitarist. Today I don't seem to care much about being anything."

Steppin nodded understandingly. "I'm sure weakening myself today," he sighed. "This heat's got me for certain. I keep yearning for it to come cool weather but then, on the other hand, when it gets cool, it will be time for school to start again. A body never knows when he is well off anyhow. When I get rich, I'm going to buy me one of those toney little steam boats like the President rides around in. Come a hot spell, I'll take my family and just sail 'em around till I find a cool spot. I'll carry them clear to the South Pole if need be."

"Say, Steppin," Pete said, "if you could reconcile yourself to missing dancing class for a couple of weeks, my dad knows a place in the country where I am going Friday, in a week, and you could go too. It's a boys' camp on a big lake. You can swim and paddle a canoe, and they feed you chicken and ice cream practically every day. And talk about cool—why you even have to sleep with two or three blankets on top of you."

"You don't say!" exclaimed Steppin. "I bet it would cost a heap of money to go there."

"Nope, that's where you're dead wrong," Pete assured him. "If you have more money than you need, you pay your own way. But if you haven't any money to spare, they take you just the same."

Steppin shook his head as though he could not believe it. "I don't see how the people that run the place can make any money that way," he protested. "Keeping kids and feeding them free chicken and ice cream every day would just about ruin any business."

"But they do," Pete insisted. "My dad says so, and he knows because—" Pete was going to say his dad knew because he had given a donation to the camp. Just in time he remembered that he had been told not to mention this. "My dad knows because the man who owns the camp said so," he finished.

"Well, it doesn't make sense, but if your dad says it's true, then I believe it," Steppin answered.

"And you will go, won't you?" Pete pleaded. "Just think, two whole weeks in the country. It would be more fun than a barrel of monkeys."

Just then they heard a din of shouting and yelling, and around the corner came a crowd of barefoot boys and girls in ragged, misfit clothes and faded bathing suits. Mr. Harrigan, the good-natured fireman from the local station, was leading them like a modern Pied Piper. Only instead of a flute, he carried a huge wrench.

"Here comes Harrigan, hurrah!" Steppin and Pete raced down the steps to join the crowd.

"Listen, Pete," Steppin said while they waited for Mr. Harrigan to unscrew the hydrant cap. "I'll be thinking over your proposition, and I'll give you my answer today right after class.

"I sure could spare the heat of this town for a spell," Steppin thought as he splashed and ran and slipped and yelled against the powerful torrent of cold water. "A fire hydrant is all right, but it's nothing like having a whole lake to cool off in." When he was back in class, sweating through the beginner routine, the idea seemed even more attractive.

"Two whole weeks!" he marveled. "I'd have to find someone to do K.P. duty for me while I was away. I wonder what Dad would say? Maybe he'd think I was ungrateful after all he's done for me, but it wouldn't do a mite of harm to ask. He can't do any more than say 'no.'

"I'll stay right here
if stay, I must,
But if I do
I'm like to bust."

Class was almost over. Steppin was humming and tapping out the last step when he noticed that Dad had limped over to the bulletin board and was printing something on it. When Steppin began to make out the words, he stopped humming and completely lost the count for his steps. Dad had written: "Come Friday, there will be no classes for two weeks on account of I'm going on my vacation."

Steppin caught Pete's eye, and with a whoop of joy, they tore out of the room.

"Can you tie that?" Steppin asked. "I was just wondering if I dare ask Dad to let me off K.P. for two weeks, and then he ups and writes that on the board. I sure am a fortunate one this day!"

"Listen, Pete," Steppin said when they had calmed down a little, "you come straight over to my house for lunch and help me tease Mom to let me go. She'll pay more heed if you come."

Since Pete and Steppin had become friends, Pete had been a daily visitor at the Stebbins' home. Mrs. Stebbins liked Pete and was always pleased to see him. He was pleasant and well-mannered with grown-ups, and he even treated Mary Ellis as if she were an important person instead of just a girl. Mary Ellis doted on him.

Steppin was quite right in thinking his mother would be more apt to let him go if Pete was there to help him persuade her. Much to his surprise, she offered no objections at all and seemed quite pleased with the idea.

As soon as they finished their lunch, the boys set off to the headquarters office of Camp Oneishta so Steppin could fill out his application. There were about a dozen boys ahead of them, and Steppin had to wait his turn. When his name was called, a young woman asked him a few questions and gave him a card to fill out. After another half hour of waiting, Steppin was given a second card and a list of instructions. He was delighted to learn that he would leave with the same group as Pete.

For the next few days, both boys were kept busy carrying out the instructions on the printed slip. First, they had to report to a clinic and be examined by a doctor. Two nurses in blue uniforms were helping the doctor. Steppin recognized one of them as Miss Walker, the Henry Street Visiting Nurse who had taken care of Mary Ellis and him when they had the measles. Miss Walker had the boys strip to their waists and gave each of them a new card. The other nurse weighed them and measured their height. Then Pete and Steppin took their places at the end of a long line of boys who were waiting to be examined.

The nurses and the doctor worked very quickly, but still it seemed a long time before their turns came. As the doctor examined each boy, he told the nurse what to write on the card and whether or not he could go to camp. When he examined Steppin's mouth, he said something about dental caries and bicuspids. Steppin was a little worried.

"Does that mean I've got to get my tonsils cut again?" he asked anxiously.

"No, Steppin, it means you must have some teeth filled before you can go to camp," Miss Walker told him. "I'll give you a note to take to the dentist."

It took two unpleasant visits to a dental clinic to get his teeth cleaned and the cavities filled. Then on Thursday, the last day before they were to leave, Pete and Steppin had to report to the office of the Henry Street Visiting Nurses for their final inspection. When all the boys were there, Miss Walker lined them up on two long benches, took their temperatures, and felt their wrists, just as if they were sick. Then, using a flashlight, she examined their throats and looked at their chests.

"She has to be sure we are not being took down with something catching like mumps or a rash," one of the boys explained.

"It sure takes a lot of bother and standing in line to get to camp, but I expect it's worth it," Steppin told Pete when they were on their way home.

"Sure, it's worth it," Pete agreed, "and anyway, we are all set now."

"All except packing our duds like it says on the list and getting ourselves to the station by noon tomorrow," Steppin sighed happily.

"That will be easy enough to do." Pete dug his hand into his pocket and produced a few coins. "Look, Steppin, I've got money enough for a soda. Let's go to the Greek's and celebrate." When, after a pleasant half hour at the ice cream parlor, they strolled out to the street, Steppin spied the lanky figure of Snakey Lewis, loitering aimlessly in front of the shop. This was the first time they had met since the day Snakey had led Butch to Dad Kirby's to lie in wait for him. Steppin considered Snakey his sworn enemy. He nudged Pete and passed Snakey without a word.

"Steppin, oh Steppin," Snakey called after them.

Steppin halted and looked back. "Well, what do you want?" he growled.

"Oh, nothing." Snakey glanced anxiously at Pete and then looked down at the pavement. "Only I don't see why you have to pass right by and disrecognize me like this."

"Why shouldn't I disrecognize you?" asked Steppin.

"Well—I was just thinking, if it would be agreeable to you, I'd be pleased to call it quits and be friends," Snakey muttered.

Steppin snorted, "Friends! So you can get a chance to sic Butch and the gang on me again, I suppose. Not much, I won't be friends with a double crosser like you."

"Honest, Steppin, I never calculated to get you in a jam, and anyway, there ain't no gang anymore."

"No gang?" Steppin couldn't hide his curiosity.

"It's like this," Snakey spoke eagerly, delighted to have Steppin's attention. "After the gang heard about the big fight, they were all down on Butch for letting himself get licked by a kid not half his size. Then Butch tries to square himself by making out he's a real genuine gangster. So, he makes little Tubby Sparks help him hold up the fruit store with a cap pistol. They had masks on just like it was a real hold-up. Only the man in the fruit store wasn't fooled, and he nabs Butch and yells out to Ted who was passing by, walking his beat. Ted spanks Tubby and sends him home, but he runs Butch in and tells his folks if he tried any more monkey business, he will have him sent to a reform school for sure. And now, none of our folks will let us mingle with Butch, no how. So that's why the gang is busted up for good."

"Say, Steppin." Snakey took a breath and changed the subject. "I saw Martie Burns, and he says you are going to the country."

"That's right," Steppin gloated. "Pete and I are all set to leave, and if you come to the One Hundred Twenty-Fifth Street Station tomorrow, you can see us get on the train and zoom away!"

"Golly, I'd admire to go to the country," Snakey sighed wistfully. "I almost went once when our Sunday school had a picnic. Then just the day before, my mother took sick, and I had to stay behind."

"That was the time his mother got taken to the hospital in the ambulance and died," Steppin remembered with a pang. He suddenly forgot all about his quarrel with Snakey.

"Golly, Snakey, I wish you were going," he said. "Only I'm afraid you're too late. Before you can even think about going, you have to have about a million cards filled out and get examinations all over town and have your bicuspids plugged, and I don't know what else."

"Yeah, I guess you're right. I wish I'd known in time, though. But that's life, I reckon."

Snakey's voice sounded trembly and hoarse and for no reason, he suddenly stooped down and fiddled with the strings of his half-laced shoe while Pete and Steppin pretended to be looking at something across the street.

"Steppin," Pete asked, "do you suppose maybe your friend, Miss Walker, could fix him up?"

"Golly, I don't know." Steppin was dubious. "We could go back and ask her, though."

"Could you, Steppin?" pleaded Snakey. "I'd sure be in your favor if you would."

"Sure, I could, Snakey. Come on, let's get going."

All the boys were gone and so was Miss Walker when the trio trudged into the office of the Henry Street Visiting Nurses. Miss Madden, the supervisor, was sitting at her desk in a little glass-enclosed office. When Steppin knocked on the open door, she looked up and smiled.

"Please, ma'am, could you tell me when Miss Walker will be back?" Steppin asked.

Miss Madden glanced at her wrist watch. "Miss Walker will be back at two o'clock to examine another group of boys. May I help you?"

"I don't know," Steppin said. "It's about my friend here, Snakey—I mean Wilbur Lewis. We want Miss Walker to fix things, so he can go to the country with us tomorrow."

"Tomorrow!" Miss Madden exclaimed. "I'm afraid that would be impossible. Perhaps we could arrange to have him go with the next group," she added kindly.

"I'd sooner go with Steppin if it's all the same to you," Snakey put in eagerly.

"But you see, there isn't enough time to get you ready," Miss Madden explained patiently.

"I'm all right to go," Snakey persisted. "You can ask Miss Carter."

"Do you mean the Miss Carter that works in this office?"

Snakey nodded. "Sure, that's right. She's got a blue dress just like yours. She's been to our house a heap of times to look us over with the things in her little black satchel. When she gets through, she writes us up on a piece of paper. She can tell you all about me."

Miss Madden went to a big file case, and after looking in one of the drawers, she came back with a cardboard folder.

"Your father's name is Wilbur, too, isn't it?" she asked. "And your mother's name is Agatha."

"That's right," Snakey nodded. "Only my mother is dead," he added softly.

"Oh, I'm sorry." Miss Madden opened the folder and began reading.

"That's it," Snakey whispered. "That's the very same piece of paper Miss Carter writes us up on with her fountain pen."

Miss Madden was reading what Miss Carter had written about the Lewis family—the poor father trying to bring up his two motherless children and run his shoe repair shop—Snakey's efforts to help out by shining shoes—the little crippled sister who would never be able to walk. She smiled very kindly at Snakey when she had finished.

"You boys sit down and wait," she told them, and she then went into her office and picked up the telephone.

While she was telephoning, Miss Walker came back. Steppin rushed up to her and blurted out his story.

"Couldn't you and your boss fix it so Snakey could go with us tomorrow?" he pleaded. "Just look at him, Miss Walker—see how sick and skinny he looks. It would do him a heap of good to go to the country."

"But the camps are for well boys," Miss Walker explained. "Sick boys go to the hospital."

Steppin laughed heartily.

"I didn't say he was sick, Miss Walker. I just said he looks kind of peaked. Why, Snakey's as strong as an ox—show Miss Walker your muscle, Snakey."

"See," he cried triumphantly as Snakey obliged by flexing his thin right arm. "Just look at that bicep! Why, a big, strong guy like him wouldn't be any bother. He could help look after the little kids."

Miss Walker turned away, and her shoulders shook as if she might be getting ready to sneeze. After a moment her shoulders stopped shaking, but when she looked at them again, her black eyes were sparkling and her pretty bronze face was twitching with suppressed amusement.

"How old are you, Wilbur?" she asked. Snakey was very tall for his age, and Steppin figured that Miss Walker might be thinking he was too old to go with their group. He decided to make him out as young as possible.

"Oh, he is around eleven years old," Steppin spoke up before Snakey could answer.

Miss Walker frowned at Steppin.

"That's too bad, Steppin. Yours is the twelve- to fourteen-year-old group. If Wilbur is only eleven, he will have to go with a ten to twelve group."

"I said *around* eleven," Steppin amended. "I reckon I sort of over-spoke myself at that. What I aimed to say was he is eleven, going on thirteen. That would make him about twelve, wouldn't it?"

"I'm thirteen and a half," Snakey ventured meekly. "You can see it on the paper Miss Carter wrote."

"That's practically what I said," Steppin defended himself.

"Oh was it!" Miss Walker frowned. "I think, Steppin, you would do better if you let Wilbur speak for himself."

"Miss Walker, may I see you for a minute?" Miss Madden called from her office.

"Why, I hope I didn't say anything wrong," Steppin said as soon as Miss Walker was out of hearing. "I was trying to fix things the best I knew how, but I would have done better if I'd just stuck to the truth. Sin never pays, I reckon."

"Well, you did your best, and come what may, I'll still be grateful to you," Snakey declared.

The three of them kept their eyes on the two nurses. Through the glass partition, they could see Miss Walker talking to Miss

Madden and using the telephone. After fifteen minutes, she came out again. She was smiling broadly.

"Wilbur, do you really want to go to the country tomorrow?" she asked.

"I sure do," Snakey assured her. "I want to go in the worst kind of way."

"Well, it just happens that there is a vacancy in tomorrow's party," Miss Walker went on. "It's too late for you to be examined by the regular camp doctor; however, we telephoned a clinic way down on East Fifty-Ninth Street that will examine you and give you a report. Do you think you could go down there?"

"Sure, he can," Steppin assured her. "Pete and I will go with him. We can start right now."

"Have you any money for carfare?" Miss Walker asked when she had written out a pink slip of paper for Snakey to give the clinic.

"No, I haven't," Snakey confessed. "But maybe I can catch a few shoe shines on the way down—unless maybe you and the boss might want to buy a shine right now," he added.

"Suppose I loan you some carfare, and you can pay me back in shoe shines later," Miss Walker suggested. "I think you had better get to the clinic as soon as possible."

"I'm much obliged to you, and as soon as I get a chance, I'll pay you back the money and give you a regular ten-cent shine for interest," Snakey promised.

A nice, long streetcar ride brought them to the clinic on East Fifty-Ninth Street. Snakey gave the note to the nurse at the desk and sat down on a bench with Steppin and Pete.

"We might as well make ourselves comfortable," Pete told Snakey. "You always have a long wait at these places."

"I'll say." Steppin sighed. "You go in these clinics a young man, and you come out old and grey and bending on a cane."

"Wilbur Lewis," the nurse called out. "This way, Wilbur, don't keep the doctor waiting."

"Well, she sure is making us out to be fibbers!" said Pete as Snakey was hustled into the examining room.

"Maybe it's because we came special and it isn't a regular clinic," Steppin suggested.

"Whatever it is, it's all right with me. Look, it's four o'clock and we haven't even had lunch."

"That's what my stomach keeps telling me," Steppin groaned.

"Well, anyway, it looks as if Snakey is going to the country."

"Here he comes now! How did you make out, Snakey?" Pete and Steppin both spoke at once.

Snakey was waving a slip of paper joyously. "I'm all set—it says so on the paper. All I have to do now is pack my things. My dad sure will be surprised," Snakey beamed as they rode back to Harlem. "Yesterday, when I told him you were going, he said he wished I could go, too."

"I think I'll get off at the corner by his shop and break the good news," Snakey decided. "And I can't tell you how much I owe for all you two have done."

"Oh, that's nothing," Pete and Steppin assured him. "So long; we'll see you at the station."

Pete got off two blocks further on and Steppin, left to himself, thought over the events of the day.

"Unless I can hold Mom off until I have time to explain, I'm going to catch it for being so late; besides which, I'm dog tired and nigh starved to death. By rights, I ought to be singing the blues for sure. Instead, I feel so happy, I could dance a triple tap from here to the Battery if need be. This morning, the last thing I would have thought of would be putting myself to any trouble for Snakey Lewis. And here I've spent my whole afternoon getting him fixed up to go to camp. I'm beginning to believe there is something to this doing kindly deeds and enjoying doing them, after all."

CHAPTER 10

Camp Oneishta

The next morning, Steppin was up before daylight. He shut off the alarm that was set to go off an hour later and tiptoed out to the kitchen. When at seven o'clock his mother came out, Steppin had washed and dressed and was packing his bag.

"My goodness, Steppin, you certainly are beforehand when you want to be," Mrs. Stebbins exclaimed.

"Well, you see, Mom, I don't want to take chances and then have to rush at the last minute."

Mrs. Stebbins chuckled. "I don't think there is much danger of that. The train isn't going to leave for nearly five hours."

Steppin assured his mother he wasn't a bit hungry, but when she told him she had planned to have hotcakes and syrup and sausages—his favorite breakfast—he changed his mind. This was the first time Steppin had ever gone away from home, and his mother and sister felt it was a very important occasion. Mary Ellis hovered over him and helped him check his traveling equipment with the printed list the camp people had given him. They packed and repacked the bag three times before they decided it was just right.

After breakfast Mary Ellis presented him with a going-away gift. It was a little embroidered billfold with a snapshot of his mother and Mary Ellis framed inside the front cover.

"I made the purse, and Virginia took the picture with her camera," Mary Ellis told him.

His mother gave him a leather toilet case completely equipped, even to a safety razor.

"I teased Mom to get one with a razor in it," confided Mary Ellis. "I think it looks right stylish to have one even if you don't need it yet."

Steppin was delighted.

"I'll say it's stylish, and having my family's pictures sure gives tone, too. Golly, I never expected you would make my going away so important," he told them.

By ten o'clock Steppin was ready to leave. He was completely dressed, even to his cap which he was wearing to keep his unruly hair slicked close to his head. He had his watch carefully pinned into his vest pocket and his new billfold in his inside coat pocket. His mother had packed his lunch in a shoe box, and there wasn't another thing to do until train time.

Steppin and Mary Ellis went out and sat on the front steps to wait for Pete and Snakey. After half an hour had passed, Steppin began to worry.

"Boy, I hope nothing has happened to them," he was saying when he saw them turn the corner, each carrying a suitcase and a lunchbox. Pete had brought his guitar also.

All three insisted they would have barely time to get to the station, so Steppin kissed his mother and Mary Ellis goodbye and gave Pedigree a farewell hug and off they went. They were the first boys to arrive. After reporting to a man sitting at a table under a sign which read "Camp Oneishta," they sat down on one of the benches reserved for their party.

"Our last wait," Steppin sighed blissfully. "Only I don't suppose we can blame this one on the camp people."

Pretty soon other boys began coming in. They were all old friends now and yelled and sang together while they waited. At three minutes to twelve, the camp counselors lined them up by twos and made them march up the stairs to the tracks. They heard the train announced through the loud speaker, and a few seconds later it thundered into the station.

Their camp party had a whole coach to itself, and Mr. Baxter, who was in charge, didn't seem to mind how much noise the boys made. After a three-hour train trip, they all piled off at a tiny station where a whole flock of station wagons were waiting to drive them out to Camp Oneishta.

It had been hot and muggy on the train. Steppin was amazed at the change as they drove along through the woods.

"When we left New York, who would have thought we would be almost cold in three hours?" he exulted.

"The lake, the lake!" Pete yelled as they rounded a bend, and there was Lake Oneishta, rippling and sparkling in the late-after-noon sunshine. They drove along the lakeshore for a few minutes, and then suddenly they were in the midst of a grove of pine trees with a dozen or more log cabins nestling among them. The station wagons drove up to the largest cabin, which had "Camp Oneishta" painted in white letters on its roof.

Coolness, sparkling water, the pungent odor of pines, and soft, velvety pine needles underfoot—these were Steppin's first impressions of Camp Oneishta.

"Boys," Mr. Baxter told them, "you can pick out your own bags, and Mr. Brown will assign you to cabins. Then if you will hurry into your bathing trunks, you will have just enough time for a dip before supper."

Snakey, Pete, and Steppin were given a cabin together along with a boy named Roy Palmer who had been to Camp Oneishta the summer before.

"Did you see that big raft out on the lake?" Pete asked as they were undressing. "Do you suppose they will let us swim out to it?"

"Not tonight they won't," Roy told him. "They never let you go in deep water until they give you a swimming test. They usually give the new boys their tests in the forenoon just before lunch."

Secretly, Pete was a little disappointed when he learned they were to take their dip in a small, enclosed space where the water was not over three feet deep. But Snakey and Steppin, whose only swimming experience was dog paddling in a city wading pool, were quite happy.

After supper they built a huge bonfire, and all sat around it. Several of the boys had musical instruments—banjos, mouth organs, horns, and mandolins. Pete brought out his guitar. They played and sang old songs like "Swing Low, Sweet Chariot" and "Old Kentucky Home" until one of the boys who had a bugle was asked to play taps.

"I'm so sleepy I can hardly walk," said Snakey when they started back to their cabin.

"So am I," Steppin yawned. "I've been up since before daybreak."

But no sooner was Steppin in bed than his sleepiness vanished. Two sides of the cabin were open except for the wire screening tacked over them. Lying in bed, the boys could look right up at the stars or at the dark outlines of the pine trees. There was no sound except the gentle lap, lap of water against the lakeshore and the soft whispering of the wind in the pines.

Presently Steppin leaned over and whispered, "Pete, are you asleep?"

"No," Pete whispered back.

Snakey sat up in bed. "Neither am I," said he.

"I'm wide awake, too," Roy chimed in from his corner. "It's always like this the first night in the country. No one can get to sleep right off. It's too quiet."

After a while, no one spoke and Steppin knew by their deep, slow breathing that they were all asleep but him. Just when he started to doze off, someone yelled, "Shove her bow offshore!" He sat up in bed and looked about him. Much to his surprise, he discovered that the voice which seemed to be yelling right in his ear came from a canoe way on the other side of the lake. He was wide awake again, and for a while he lay listening to the voices. When the canoe had carried them out of hearing, he tried to go to sleep, but it was no use.

"Golly, it's so still and lonesome, it's giving me the spooks," he confessed to himself. "I can almost hear the quiet tipping around."

A golden glow appeared in the sky, and pretty soon the moon came up, turning the darkness into silvery light. Steppin recalled having heard someone say that if people slept with the moonlight shining on them, they would be crazy when they awakened. "If there is any truth in it, we'll all be raving lunatics," he thought. "I wonder how long it will be until morning.

"I wish Mr. Brown hadn't taken my watch to lock it up in the safe. It's going to be a powerful long time waiting till daybreak with nothing to do but lie here with the moon staring right at me while I keep wondering what time it is."

The next thing he knew, the moon began getting bigger and brighter and started falling toward him. It fell faster and faster, getting hotter and brighter every second. Steppin tried to scream, but he couldn't make a sound. Just when it was about two inches from his nose, someone blew a blast on a trumpet and Steppin sat up and opened his eyes. It was broad daylight and the morning sun was shining right in his eyes. The trumpet blast was the bugler blowing reveille.

Everyone had another dip in the pool before breakfast. Then, after the camp had been put to rights, they all gathered at the dock for the swimming tests.

"Swimmers and divers at this end; beginners and non-divers at the far end," the swimming instructor ordered.

Snakey promptly trotted down to the beginner's end. Steppin, who had never dived in his life, was just about to follow him when he noticed that Pete had taken a place in the line-up at the diving board. Steppin stepped into place behind him.

"I reckon if a little fellow like Pete isn't afraid to dive, I'm not afraid either," thought Steppin. "Besides, I'm not going to join up with all those little kids."

He watched with some apprehension as the first boy walked out on the plank and plunged into the water.

"Not bad," the instructor commented.

"It looks pretty easy at that," Steppin reassured himself. The second boy didn't do so well. He sprawled through the air with his arms and legs waving like a windmill and sent up an enormous splash when he hit the water. When he swam back, the instructor told him, "No diving without further instructions."

"Say, Pete," asked Steppin casually, "have you done much diving?"

"Oh, sure," Pete assured him. "I've been swimming and diving ever since I was four years old. In Haiti I never missed a day all the year round."

"Oh." Steppin suddenly wished with all his heart he had had sense enough to go with Snakey.

"Well, it's too late for that," he sighed, "all I can do now is study Pete and try to copy what he does."

It was Pete's turn. Steppin watched him intently as he stood poised at the end of the board and bounced it lightly. Then, like a flash, Pete's feet flipped up in the air, and Pete had cut into the water with hardly a splash.

"Nice work, Bergeret," the instructor praised him. "All right, Stebbins, hop to it."

Steppin drew himself erect as Pete had done and walked

briskly out on the diving board. From the dock, it looked quite low, but when Steppin stood at the end of the board and looked down, it seemed a long way from the water.

He dared not hesitate for he knew that if he did, he would surely lose his nerve; so, closing his eyes tightly, he threw himself into the water. The next instant, he felt something strike the entire front of his body a stinging blow.

"Golly, I must have hit a rock or something," he spluttered as he struggled and thrashed in the cold water.

Someone grabbed the seat of his trunks and dragged him to shore.

"Are you hurt?" the instructor asked as he hauled Steppin up on the dock.

"No, sir—that is, not much, sir," Steppin gasped.

"I thought I said divers were to come to this end, Stebbins. Did you by any chance think you knew how to dive?"

"Well, you see, I never dove before, so I wasn't sure whether I knew how or not. I thought the best way to find out if I could dive was to try," Steppin explained.

"I hope you know now," the instructor said sternly. "Get down to the far end with the beginners."

"Yes, sir."

Although Steppin did not look up, he was aware of the amused glances of the other boys; and as he walked away, he heard some of them laugh out loud.

"Golly, anyone would think I'd learn some sense," he sighed. "Why do I always have to make a fool of myself, trying to do something I don't know anything about? I should have learned a lifelong lesson that time I had the brass to tell Bob Williams I knew how to dance. But no, I just keep on and on."

"Have you changed your mind, Stebbins?" Mr. Foster, the beginners' instructor, greeted him.

"I sure have," Steppin declared. "I reckon there is more to this diving stuff than I figured. I'd like to learn it, though," he added eagerly.

"Well, you certainly don't mind trying, and that's something," Mr. Foster consoled him.

Except for the good-natured jibes of his companions about his ridiculous diving performance, Steppin's two weeks at camp were a period of perfect pleasure. He took his diving and swimming almost as seriously as his dancing, and he was pleased at the progress he made.

Living, eating, and sleeping in the open was a delightful novelty to all, but Snakey enjoyed it even more than the others. "I never knew it would be like this," he marveled. "Boy, when I grow up, I'm going to scheme up some way so I can live in the country all the year round. Maybe I'll be a farmer."

"It isn't like this all the year round," Roy told him. "I lived on a farm once and come winter, it's as cold and lonesome as anything. The snow heaps up almost to the top of your house, and you have to shovel a new path practically every day. Besides, you have to chop wood and split kindling and do all kinds of chores."

"I wouldn't care so long as I knew I'd be right on the spot when summer came into sight," Snakey declared.

They were always hungry, and although they didn't have chicken and ice cream every day, as Pete had predicted, no one even noticed the omissions. Everything tasted a thousand times better than it had at home, and even food which ordinarily they didn't care for seemed amazingly appetizing. Steppin ate, with gusto, mashed turnips, which he had always detested. Pete had never liked fish, but when a speckled lake trout he caught himself was cooked for him, he declared he had never tasted anything half as good.

Early in the second week, everyone began getting ready for Stunt Night, which was to be held on their last evening. The boys in each cabin were supposed to do something on the program. Stunt Night was quite an occasion, and many of the camp sponsors came all the way from New York to attend.

Steppin, Pete, Roy, and Snakey planned a little number

together. Steppin was to do a tap dance accompanied on the guitar by Pete. Snakey was to give an exhibition of his famous trick of kicking the back of his head with both feet at once. Pete was to play a guitar solo, and Roy was to sing a vocal solo in which they would all join in on the chorus.

Steppin felt a little uneasy about attempting a solo. He hadn't danced before an audience since the closing exercises at school; and ever since he had seen Bob Williams dance at the Lafayette, Steppin had had a very modest opinion of his own ability. He confessed his misgivings to Pete.

"Well, Steppin, you are no professional yet, but you're not bad. I even heard Dad Kirby talking about you to Bob Williams one day, and guess what he said?"

"Something about my dancing?" Steppin asked eagerly. "What did he say?"

"To tell the truth, I wasn't going to mention it because I didn't want you to get a swelled head," Pete said frankly.

"Spill it, Pete. I won't get a swelled head, cross my heart!"

"All right then. I heard Dad tell Bob you were one of the most promising kids in the school."

Steppin's eyes sparkled, and a grin lit his brown face. "Did he really say that? Golly, Pete, I sure am in your favor for telling me, and it's not because I want to get puffed up or anything, either. You see, I've just got to make good as a dancer."

"That's why I figured maybe I ought to tell you," Pete exclaimed. "Besides, I thought it would help put your mind to rest about dancing on Stunt Night."

"It sure helps," Steppin nodded. As the great night drew near, the rehearsals began in earnest. Since the boys in each cabin were trying to keep their stunts secret from the others, the pine woods were dotted with little groups practicing; and snatches of songs and the music of mandolins, banjos, and mouth organs could be heard every afternoon.

Pete and Steppin, who were in charge of their skit, were well pleased with the talent their cabin had to offer. "After all, we can all do something," Pete commented. "Roy has a right good voice. Steppin's no slouch of a dancer. I can strum a guitar, and Snakey here has a real stunt he can do."

"I wish I could do something more," Snakey confessed. "Just kicking my head isn't much of a stunt when you put it up against what you fellows are doing."

"Maybe it isn't much when you can do it, but you are the only one I ever knew who could," Pete comforted him.

On the day before the performance, each group gave a private rehearsal for the camp counselors. They seemed quite impressed with the skit Pete and Steppin had arranged. Later, when the program was made up, the boys were delighted to find that theirs was the final number.

"We are the dessert," Steppin exclaimed, "the best place of all."

Supper was an hour earlier on Stunt Night so there would be ample time for everyone to get ready for the performance, which was to start promptly at seven. Steppin, Pete, Snakey, and Roy, since they had no costumes to prepare, spent the afternoon helping decorate the assembly hall with branches of pine and hemlock. Then, after supper, when carloads of visitors began to arrive, the four were detailed to show them over the camp.

When the assembly hall was filled, the groups of boys took their places in the first two rows so that they could get to the stage easily. The first four boys on the program played "Yankee Doodle" on homemade instruments. One played on a saw, one on a comb, another on a cigar-box banjo, and the fourth boy played a drum made by stretching a piece of leather over a mixing bowl. Other groups sang quartets, whistled together, did tumbling and acrobatics, or played musical instruments. Since no group was allowed more than fifteen minutes for its stunt, the program moved quickly. When the next to the last number, an excellent tumbling act, was being given, Pete, Steppin, Roy, and Snakey were waiting in the wings. The tumblers finished by standing four deep on each other's shoulders. After they had

been warmly applauded and called back to bow again to the
audience, Steppin walked out to introduce their stunt.

"Ladies, gentlemen, and fellow campers," he greeted them, "we
are about to offer, for your pleasure, some music by Pete Bergeret
who plays the guitar and is a first-class fighter besides; a song by
Roy Palmer who has a real church voice; and a stunt by Snakey
Lewis which I've never seen done by any other boy. I am going
to do a tap dance. I'm not nearly as good a dancer as I aim to be
someday, but I hope my dancing is a little better than my diving."

All the boys and the counselors laughed heartily at Steppin's reference to his diving. Steppin laughed, too, and after
bowing to Pete, who came on with his guitar, he walked back
to the wings. Pete played "Cielito Lindo" with variations. After
acknowledging the applause that rewarded his fine playing,
Pete sat down again and strummed a few bars of "Kitten on the
Keys," which was the music for Steppin's dance.

As he came out, Steppin's old stage fright swept over him, but
after the first few steps he began to enjoy the thrill of dancing
before an audience. When he slid easily and confidently into a
difficult step, everyone started clapping and kept right on until
the dance was over. "Boy, that was worth all the time and bother
I put in, learning that step," Steppin thought as he came back to
make his bow.

Then Pete struck a note on the guitar, and Snakey stepped
out. While Pete played up the scale, Snakey kicked the back of
his head with both feet, one kick for each note. He had timed
it so the eight jumps carried him clear across the stage. This
was Snakey's only outstanding talent. He had practiced it for
years and could do it with a careless ease which seemed to defy
gravity. Steppin and Roy were delighted at the enthusiasm with
which Snakey was greeted. When Snakey reached the far side of
the stage, Pete played a descending scale, and Snakey re-crossed
the stage backward, kicking his head with each leap as easily as
he had done it going forward.

"You sure knocked them cold," Roy and Steppin told him when, on the final note, Snakey joined them in the wings.

Pete began playing again, and all three came out and stood behind him. Roy sang,

> "Sometimes I feel like a motherless child,
> Sometimes I feel like a motherless child,
> Sometimes I feel like a motherless child,"

Then all together, they crooned,

> "A long way from home."

When they were just practicing together, Steppin hadn't realized how well Roy sang. Now, as his clear tenor voice rang out, Steppin was so moved he almost forgot to join in with the others on the final line. He began thinking about his mother and Mary Ellis and funny old Pedigree and what good times they had together in their railroad flat in Harlem. He was just trying to picture what they would be doing now when the audience started clapping, and he came to with a start and realized their skit was finished.

When they came out of the hall, the camp fires were lighted. They spent the rest of the evening toasting frankfurters and marshmallows on long sticks over the glowing coals. Everyone kept congratulating everyone else on the success of the stunts. The counselors and visitors, too, praised their efforts. It was a jolly, happy evening and one which all of them would long remember.

The next morning all was hustle and confusion. "Golly," Snakey sighed when they were finally on the tram. "If I could have my father and sister here, I'd like to never have to leave this place."

"Oh, I don't know," said Steppin, "I was crazy to get here, and I liked every minute I was here. But now I'm just as excited about getting back to Harlem."

As the train sped along, Steppin began singing to himself:

> "North or South
> Shut my mouth

> East or West
> Harlem's best."

He chanted softly, keeping in time with the ceaseless rhythm of the wheels.

When the train finally entered New York City, his spirits rose higher and higher. A few minutes later, he was looking down upon the familiar streets of Harlem, and he could no longer control his excitement.

> "North or South
> Shut my mouth
> East or West
> Harlem's best."

He shouted and instantly all the boys took up the chant.

"Hurray for Harlem—good old Harlem!" they yelled as the train pulled into the One Hundred and Twenty-Fifth Street station.

After they were off the train, it seemed to Steppin that the counselors were never going to let him go home. The younger boys' parents were there to meet them, and everybody had to line up and be checked off the list. Then the boys shook hands all around and said goodbye.

Nearly an hour later, Steppin hopped off a bus two blocks from his house.

> "East or West
> Home is best."

He hummed happily as he ran up Eighth Avenue. When he turned the corner, the first person he saw was Mary Ellis, waiting at the top of their basement steps.

"He's coming," she yelled, and by the time he got to the door, his mother was there to greet him.

Then Pedigree came racing in from the kitchen. He rushed and threw himself at Steppin again and again, barking his noisy welcome.

"My, it sure is nice to be home again," Steppin told them when Pedigree had quieted down and they were settled in the kitchen dining car.

"I wanted Mom and me to meet you at the train, but she figured we'd better stay home and have your supper ready," Mary Ellis said.

"I'm hungry, all right," Steppin confessed, "and it sure is a good supper—pork chops, yams and gravy, and mustard greens—everything I like best!"

"And a deep apple pie for dessert," Mrs. Stebbins informed him.

After supper Steppin called at the laundry to spend a few minutes with Charley Kee. Then Mrs. Stebbins and Mary Ellis had to hear about all he had seen and done at Camp Oneishta. Afterward they told him everything that had happened while he was away. It was nearly midnight before they even thought of going to bed.

"How ever did it get so late without me noticing?" Mrs. Stebbins scolded.

"At least we have a few days to catch up on our sleep," Mary Ellis reminded her mother. "And Monday is Labor Day."

"But the day after Labor Day is the first day of school," Steppin sighed. "Only I've had such a prime summer, I don't mind going back nearly as much as I thought I would."

CHAPTER 11

Mary Ellis Has a Birthday Party

On Tuesday, Steppin went back to school and resumed his dancing classes and kitchen police duties at Dad Kirby's. The dancing classes were held in the afternoon now, and each class met only three times a week. Still, it was the busiest fall and winter Steppin had ever known.

Although he had been promoted to Dad's advanced class before his vacation, he attended nearly every session of the beginners' class. Two afternoons a week, he stayed after class to clean the studio. What with the homework he had to do for school and helping High Pockets with the janitor work, it seemed to Steppin he almost never had a minute to call his own. At night he was so tired he seldom teased his mother to let him go out and play under the street lights.

Friday evenings and Saturday afternoons were the high spots of each week. On Saturdays, as soon as Steppin finished his janitor chores, he and Pete went to the Bergeret Boxing School and amused themselves playing with the punching bags and gymnasium apparatus. Then, too, watching the professional boxers work and talking to them was a pleasant pastime.

Friday evenings, Pete usually had supper with the Stebbins family, and, as likely as not, Roy and Snakey would drop in later. Usually Virginia Day came to spend the evening with Mary Ellis. As soon as the supper dishes were done, Pete would get out his guitar and Mary Ellis would settle down at the organ. Then, until the clock struck ten, the five of them would make the house ring as they played and sang and danced. And sometime during the evening, the boys always put on their stunt just as they had done it at Camp Oneishta.

Often Pete would play the organ. He declared that pumping the floor boards and working the hand valves was much more fun than playing a piano. But Mary Ellis still yearned for a real piano with all the keys working.

"My, I'd admire to play like you do," she confided to Pete one evening. "I reckon taking lessons costs a heap of money," she added wistfully.

"My mother taught me music for my first four years," Pete explained. "Now I go to a teacher way down on West Fifty-Seventh Street. I think he does charge quite a lot."

Mary Ellis shook her head. "I guess I'll just have to keep in patience until Steppin becomes a famous dancer before I can ever take lessons. But I surely do pine to do so," she sighed.

Just then Mrs. Stebbins and Virginia Day came in with a plate of hot fudge. When they had eaten every crumb of it and were ready to leave, Mary Ellis invited all of them to her birthday supper on Saturday of the following week.

"It isn't my true birthday until Tuesday, in a week," she confessed. "But Mom always has us celebrate on a Saturday whether it's the right day or not."

All the way home, Pete kept thinking about Mary Ellis and how she longed to take music lessons. His mother was alone when he came in, and it suddenly occurred to Pete that she might give Mary Ellis lessons just as she had given them to him.

"I would be most happy to help this little girl, Pierre," she said after he had told her his story. "But if she has no piano and only an old, worn-out organ for practicing, I'm afraid she would make little progress."

Pete realized that his mother was right, but still he kept thinking how nice it would be if there were some way he could help Mary Ellis. It would please Mrs. Stebbins and Steppin, too, and all of them had been so good to him.

On the following Friday, he was idly glancing over the weekly Amsterdam News when he saw an item that made his eyes bulge with excitement.

"Will give upright piano to any reliable person who will call for same," he read. "If interested, apply in person to L. G. Carter, 290 St. Nicholas Terrace."

It seemed almost too good to be true. Pete's fingers trembled as he tore out the notice. Without a word to anyone, he skipped out of the house and hurried to Dad Kirby's to consult with Steppin. Steppin, too, was overjoyed at the prospect of getting a free piano for Mary Ellis.

"We'll get them to deliver it tomorrow," he told Pete. "Boy, oh, boy, what a birthday gift that's going to be!"

"Do you know where St. Nicholas Terrace is?" Pete asked.

"Sure I do. It's up on Sugar Hill. I know right about where that number is, too. I've delivered plenty of laundry up there. We better go right off now before they give it to someone else."

"I wonder why they call this 'Sugar Hill'?" Pete asked as they trudged along the sidewalk.

"That's easy. It's because the black folks who live here are so rich they don't have to eat anything but sugar unless they want to," Steppin explained.

"I should think they'd call it 'Candy Hill' instead of 'Sugar Hill,'" Pete protested. "Candy is a heap better than sugar."

"That's right, too. However, they both are good—here we are," Steppin interrupted himself. "It's a right nice place, too," he approved as they peered through a huge iron gate at a modern apartment house built around a garden courtyard like a medieval monastery. "The Cloisters" was written in bronze letters over the gate.

"Some people think these churchy-looking places are even more toney than Striver's Row," Steppin told Pete as they studied the list of tenants' names. "But not me! To my mind they're not a patch on having a whole house to yourself and a brass plate with only your own name on it."

He pressed the button marked "L. G. Carter." When the lock clicked, Pete turned the big knob on the gate and they stepped inside. The gate had hardly closed behind them when the bright blue door of Apartment 3 opened, and a pleasant-looking dark-skinned man in a red moire dressing gown looked out.

Pete snatched off his cap. "Is this where Mr. Carter lives?" he asked, politely.

"That's right," the man replied, taking a puff on the pipe he was holding. "I'm Carter."

"My name is Manuel Pierre Bergeret," Pete introduced himself. "And this is my friend, Steppin A. Stebbins."

"Bergeret?" Mr. Carter took his pipe out of his mouth. "Any relation to Mannie Bergeret, the boxer?"

"Yes, sir, he's my dad," Pete told him.

"Well, now, isn't that something," Mr. Carter smiled. "And what can I do for you?"

"We've come to ask about the piano you are giving away," Pete told him.

"We thought, like as not, there was some mistake," Steppin spoke up. "It doesn't make sense that anyone would up and give a piano away free. But Pete, here—I mean, Pierre and I figured it wouldn't do a mite of harm to find out about it."

"No, there is no mistake. My wife's mother is giving her a baby grand, and she would rather give away the one she has than sell it for next to nothing. But what puzzles me is why you boys want a piano. Come on in and tell me about it."

Mr. Carter led them into a beautifully furnished living room. "It's like this, sir," Pete explained. "Steppin's little sister, Mary Ellis, wants to study piano playing the worst kind of way. I've got it all fixed up that my mother will give her lessons, if we can get a piano for her to practice on."

"So when we saw by the paper how you were giving away a piano, we came right on up," Steppin put in eagerly.

"You see," Pete finished, "tomorrow is Mary Ellis' birthday, and we want the piano for a big surprise at her party."

"Well, that sounds all right," Mr. Carter announced after he had asked them a few questions about Mary Ellis and the Stebbins family.

He nodded toward a small, cottage-size piano standing against the wall behind them. "There it is, boys, and it's all yours."

"Boy, isn't that neat!" Steppin exclaimed.

They got up and went over to admire the piano more closely.

"She's got a shine that puts the noon day sun to shame," Steppin beamed. "I bet Mary Ellis' eyes will bug right out of her head when she casts them on this baby."

"She certainly is just about perfect, and we sure are in your favor for letting us have her," Pete said earnestly.

"Oh, that's all right," Mr. Carter assured them. "The next question is, have you boys enough money to pay for having the piano moved?"

"Money to pay for having the piano moved!" For a minute the boys were speechless. They had just taken it for granted that the Carters would deliver the piano for them.

"About how much does it cost to move a piano?" Steppin tried not to sound as dismayed as he felt.

"What floor do you live on?" Mr. Carter asked.

"Basement," Steppin told him.

"Well, that's good. With only a few steps at that end and none at all here, it shouldn't cost more than ten or fifteen at the most."

"Ten or fifteen dollars!" Steppin turned away to hide his disappointment.

After a long pause, Pete spoke up.

"Oh, we can manage that easy enough. Will it be all right if we send someone for it the first thing in the morning?"

"Sure, the sooner the better," Mr. Carter nodded. "I won't be here, but the maid will let them in. By the way, what is your dad doing now?"

Pete told Mr. Carter about his father's boxing school, and then after thanking him again for the piano, the boys left.

"Only ten or fifteen dollars," Steppin groaned as soon as they were out on the street. "Golly, Pete, wouldn't you know there would have to be a catch like that somewhere? I'm right glad you pretended that we would send someone for it, though. I'd hate to have Mr. Carter know that we were dumb enough to think he'd pay for moving it."

"Listen, Steppin, I wasn't just pretending, or at least, not altogether. When he first let out about our paying to have it moved, I was so flabbergasted I didn't know what to say. Then I got to thinking—it isn't a very big piano—Steppin," Pete broke off, "You don't suppose we could move it ourselves, do you?"

"Hot diggity, that's an idea!" Steppin stared admiringly at Pete. "Maybe we could get it over to my house, Pete, but however would we carry it down our basement stairs?"

"Well," Pete explained, "I figured if we got it that far, maybe someone would help us."

"There's something in that, too. Harmon's Moving and Express business is just three doors down from our house," Steppin remembered. "But old Harmon just naturally hates everybody and especially kids," he added gloomily. "But like you say, there surely ought to be *someone* who would lend us a hand."

"Roy is awfully big for his age," Pete was thinking out loud. "We could get him to dress up in some of his father's clothes and go with us. The Carter's maid wouldn't know but what he was a sure enough moving man."

"And we can get Snakey to come along and help us," said Steppin. "You know, Pete, I wouldn't wonder if by tomorrow night that little old piano would be shining away right in my own parlor."

Early the next forenoon, a strange procession trudged up to Mr. Carter's apartment on Sugar Hill. It was headed by Roy, wearing his father's overalls and a faded blue shirt. He had a square of burlap tied around his waist as an apron, and he carried an old khaki blanket over one arm. Next came tall, lanky Snakey who, too, was wearing overalls and a burlap apron. He carried a coiled clothesline. To make himself look more grown up, Snakey had glued a tiny black mustache over his upper lip.

"Golly, Snakey, your own father wouldn't know you," Steppin declared.

It was true that Snakey's appearance was changed. However, instead of making him appear older, the dab of black on his light-brown face was so out of keeping with his childish features that he looked rather ridiculous. Pete and Steppin wore long pants but did not try to disguise their age. Their cue was to keep out of sight until Roy and Snakey had the piano safely out of the Carter's apartment.

The iron gate of The Cloisters was open, and a moving van was backed up to the curb.

"How great!" Steppin exclaimed. "Now the maid will think we belong with the van."

After a whispered last-minute rehearsal, Roy and Snakey swaggered up to Apartment 3 and rang the bell.

"We've come to get the piano for Mr. Stebbins," Roy growled in the deep bass voice he had practiced.

Outside the gate, Pete and Snakey held their breath until they heard the maid answer, "Right this way." Then they waited anxiously, watching the open door of Number 3.

"What if they can't budge it?" Steppin fretted. "Oh, boy, I wish they would come."

After what seemed a very long time, they heard a heavy rumbling and squeaking, and presently the blanket-covered piano moved into sight. As soon as Roy and Snakey had pushed it into the court, Pete and Steppin came to their aid. The maid followed them to the door and stood watching them as they slowly shoved the piano across the courtyard. The moving van which was still backed up to the curb seemed to dispel any misgivings she had, for, to their relief, they heard her slam the door just as they started through the gateway.

Two huge men came out of another apartment, carrying a davenport, and had to wait until the boys had shoved the piano out to the sidewalk. They stopped grumbling and looked puzzled when the boys turned the piano about and started to push it down the street. A few passersby stopped and stared at them. But the boys were so relieved to have the piano in their possession, and so occupied with the business of moving it, that they were unaware of everything else.

"If we can get it down off the sidewalk at the crossing, we'll be all right," Roy puffed. "After that, we can run it on the street all the way home."

Sliding the piano off the curb to the street was not nearly as difficult as they had anticipated. Their next problem was to steer it down the steep hill from St. Nicholas Terrace to Eighth Avenue. Snakey tied his rope around it, and then Roy gave them their directions.

"Now, Steppin, you and Pete keep behind and pull back on the rope with all your might and main. Snakey and I will keep in front and do likewise. Get all set and on the next green light, we will let her go."

They turned the piano so that one end was headed toward the foot of the hill. When the traffic light changed to green, Steppin and Pete braced themselves and clutched the rope while Roy and Snakey gave it a gentle shove. The piano started rolling.

"All right, let's go," Roy sang out. "Hold back, hold back!" he shouted as the piano began rolling faster and faster.

The four of them were pulling back with all their strength, but still they had to run to keep up with the piano. Steppin was sure his arms would be pulled off any minute, and the rope was burning his hands so badly that he could scarcely keep them clenched. Pete, too, was having a bad time. But even so, their task was easier than that of Roy and Snakey who were almost in front of the piano. Faster and faster they went toward the intersection at the foot of the hill. They crossed the intersection just as the light changed. Half way down the next block, the piano began moving more and more slowly and finally it stopped. The boys eased it close to the curb and sat down to get their breath and rest their aching arms before starting on the last lap of their journey.

From now on they had only the heavy Eighth Avenue traffic to trouble them, and in a few minutes, they had the piano parked at the curb in front of Steppin's basement home.

Dozens of children gathered around them, besieging them with questions. All up and down the block, grown-ups leaned out of windows to watch them. Mr. Harmon took his feet down from the iron courtyard railing of his Moving and Express office and whirled around in his swivel chair to see what was going on. Charley Kee came hurrying out of the laundry, wiping his steamy glasses to get a better look at the strange sight.

"What you up to, Steppin?" he scolded.

Briefly, Steppin explained. "Are Mom and Mary Ellis still out?" he asked. Mr. Kee nodded.

"I think they come home pretty quick now," he told Steppin.

"Golly, I hope we can get it in the parlor before they get back," Steppin said. "Here comes old Harmon, but it's no use asking him to give us a hand."

Mr. Harmon strolled slowly toward the group of chattering children and stood with his arms folded, scowling down at the four boys. Mr. Kee pattered over and stood beside him.

"These foolish youths think they will try to carry the little piano down the steps," he confided sadly.

"I'll say they are fools!" Mr. Harmon agreed scornfully.

"That's what I try to tell them," Charley sighed. "I say to them that it would need ten men even of the great strength of you to do this feat."

"Ten men to carry that little music box?" Mr. Harmon spat contemptuously. "Give me one more good man, and I could carry it to the top of the Statue of Liberty."

Mr. Kee's little almond eyes became almost round with amazement. He looked over the crowd and sighted Buck Norman, a strapping young fellow who helped his father in his ice and coal business.

"You say you and one other strong man such as Buck could do this feat?" he asked incredulously. Buck shoved his way through the crowd.

"Sure, we could, couldn't we, Harmon?" he bragged. Mr. Kee looked so doubtful that the crowd of boys and girls became impressed by the difficulty of the task.

"Sure they could move it. I bet anything they could," some of them began saying.

"I bet you three to one they couldn't," others protested.

Mr. Kee spread his small hands helplessly and shook his head. "I'll take your word, Mr. Harmon. I do not wish you or our young Buck to be hurt to prove that you can do this feat."

Buck threw out his chest and swaggered up to the piano.

"Oh, come on, Harmon, let's show Mr. Kee what a couple of real he-men can do."

"Okay," Harmon laughed.

The crowd of children became silent, watching intently as the two men lifted the piano over the sidewalk and slowly maneuvered it down the steep narrow steps.

"What did I tell you? I knew they could do it! Hurrah for Buck and Harmon," they chattered and shouted as the men set the piano down in the areaway.

"Well, what do you think of that, Charley?" Buck chaffed the little laundry man.

Mr. Kee folded his arms in his sleeves and bowed low to hide the twinkle in his eyes.

"I have seen a miracle," he declared solemnly.

The boys had just time to install the piano in the parlor and move the organ out to the caboose before Mrs. Stebbins and Mary Ellis returned. Steppin met them at the door.

"Mom, we boys have the parlor all set for a little surprise we cooked up for the party," he explained. "So will you and Mary Ellis keep out of there until after supper?"

"I only hope you haven't made a mess in the parlor," Mrs. Stebbins told Steppin when he came in for lunch.

Steppin slid into his place at the table and stretched his legs wearily.

"I'd sure hate to work as hard as I have this morning just making a mess," he grinned.

Mary Ellis and Virginia Day spent the afternoon getting ready for the party. As Mary Ellis' birthday was in the last week of October, she always used fall decorations. When her guests arrived, the long kitchen table, covered with orange and brown crepe paper, looked very festive. The centerpiece was a pumpkin. The drop light over the table, covered with orange crepe paper, cast a soft glow over the room.

When the time to reveal their wonderful surprise drew near, the boys could hardly wait. They kept whispering to each other and exchanging mysterious remarks until Mary Ellis became so curious she declared she must see what was in the parlor before she could ever cut her birthday cake. As all of them had taken the edge off their appetites with several hot dogs each, potato salad, doughnuts, sweet potato pie, and quantities of sweet cider, they decided this would be a very good plan. But, first of all, they insisted that she must open the packages beside her plate.

The boys watched impatiently while Mary Ellis exclaimed over a little bottle of perfume which Virginia had brought her and a manicure set which her mother had given her. But when she picked up a large white envelope and opened it, they were all attention.

Mary Ellis' pretty brown face shone with pleasure as she read the letter enclosed.

"Oh, Mom, listen to this:

> Dear Mary Ellis,
> Pierre tells me that you'd like very much to study piano music. This little note is to wish you a happy birthday and to tell you I shall be most happy to give you lessons. Would you like to commence Monday after school?
>
> Sincerely yours,
> Pierre's mother, Gregoire Bergeret

"Oh, Pete, you teased your mother to give me music lessons; I know you did! So it's really a birthday gift from you. I just couldn't ever have had a gift I wanted more. I'm going to practice my head off even if the old organ gets so bad not one of the keys plays. You see if I don't, Mom!"

"I know you will do your very best, honey," Mrs. Stebbins smiled, "and we hardly know how to thank you and your mother, Pete," she told him warmly.

"You still have another letter to look at, Mary Ellis," Snakey urged. Mary Ellis opened the second envelope.

> "We have hidden a little gift in the parlor. Find it and it's yours. Signed, 'The Oneishta Four.'"

"You all come with me," Mary Ellis begged when she finished reading their mysterious note. "And while I'm searching, you boys have to tell me if I'm hot or cold."

"No, ma'am!" they declared as they solemnly trailed after her, "you've got to find it your own self, even if it takes you all night."

"Oh, dear, I'm so poor at finding things like that," she protested as she led them into the dark parlor, "sometimes when we play Hide the Thimble, I can't see it even when it's right under my nose."

"Like as not, you'll be a great grandma before you find this thimble," Roy assured her, and all of them roared with laughter.

"Goodness, I can't even find the light," Mary Ellis declared as she swept her arm over her head, trying to locate the bulb. She finally found it and turned on the light.

"As soon as my eyes stop blinking, I'm going to start hunting in this corner and go right smack around the room—" Just then Mary Ellis saw the piano. "Oh!" she caught her breath.

For a whole minute, she stood twisting her brown fingers and staring at the piano. Then she turned to her mother, who was clutching the door knob and looking as if her knees were about to collapse under her.

"Mom, Mom!" Mary Ellis ran to her mother and, hiding her face in her apron, began to sob.

"There, there, honey, don't cry." Mrs. Stebbins sank weakly into an arm chair and gathered Mary Ellis to her breast. Virginia Day, round-eyed, watched cautiously from the adjoining room, as if she feared the piano might charge at her any minute. After the first shock of Mary Ellis' unaccountable behavior, Roy, Pete, and Snakey looked to Steppin for an explanation.

"Mom, doesn't she even like it?" Steppin demanded.

"Like it! Of course she likes it. But she is overcome, and so am I," Mrs. Stebbins added.

Mary Ellis turned her tear-stained face toward Steppin.

"I love it," she sobbed.

"It's only natural for her to cry," Mrs. Stebbins declared. "She is too happy, that's all. Mary Ellis, you must dry your tears, now, or the boys will think you are feeling badly. You know how funny boys are."

"How funny boys are!" Steppin snorted. "Maybe they are funny, but I never saw a boy bawling because he was happy!"

Mary Ellis sat up and blinked away her tears. "I never was so happy in my whole livelong life," she declared solemnly.

It took considerable reassurance from Mrs. Stebbins and Mary Ellis before the crest-fallen boys could be made to believe that Mary Ellis' tears were really an expression of perfect happiness.

"And now, if you don't mind, I'd be pleased to know how this piano got here," Mrs. Stebbins suggested when tranquility was restored.

Mrs. Stebbins, Mary Ellis, and Virginia listened with flattering attention while the boys, all talking at once, gave them the piano's history from the moment Pete had seen the notice in the newspaper.

"Except for Pete, we would never have known about it," Steppin said.

"Yes, but if it hadn't been for Roy and Snakey helping us, we never could have moved it," Pete put in.

"And if it hadn't been for Charley Kee, Mary Ellis would have had to sit right out on the street to practice her scales," Roy reminded them.

As it was growing late, Mrs. Stebbins suggested it was time to cut the birthday cake.

"I'm going to cut it right in here, so I can look at my piano while I'm eating," Mary Ellis insisted. "And, Mom, will you and Virginia please get things ready and light the candles? I'm going to invite Mr. Kee to my party," she declared.

Mrs. Stebbins and Virginia covered the parlor center table with a white napkin and brought in the cake. When Mary Ellis came back with Mr. Kee, the pink candles were lighted and the room light was turned out.

"Before I blow out the candles, I'm going to make a wish that every one of you will always be as happy as I am tonight," Mary Ellis told them. "And if I blow them all out with one puff, it will come true for sure."

She took a big breath and blew as hard as she could, and every candle light went out.

"Didn't I tell you my wish would be true?" she exclaimed. "Now, let's cut the cake."

Mr. Kee seemed to be enjoying the party as much as anyone. He sat quietly, smiling about him while the boys again told how, by some miracle, he had persuaded Buck and the surly Mr. Harmon to carry the piano down the steps.

"I think you were wonderful, Mr. Kee," Mary Ellis told him as he rose to leave. "How ever did you make that mean old Mr. Harmon come to it?"

Mr. Kee raised his hand and pointed his thin index finger upward.

"'He who flatters the vain man has a willing servant,'" he quoted, smiling gravely down at Mary Ellis.

"What was he talking about?" asked Snakey when Mr. Kee had bowed himself out.

"Oh, Charley is always saying things like that," explained Steppin.

"There is a lot of truth in what he said," Mrs. Stebbins reflected.

"That's true," agreed Roy. "He's right smart!"

"I'll say he is. If you ask me, he couldn't be any smarter, even if he had been born and grown up right here in Harlem," Steppin declared.

CHAPTER 12

Steppin Tries His Wings

One afternoon early in January, Dad Kirby kept the advanced dancers after class to make an announcement. Steppin knew from Dad's serious expression that he was going to say something important. After calling for order, Dad perched himself on his high stool and rested his chin on the arm piece of his crutch.

"Boys," he began, "I've set the fifteenth of February as the date for our yearly recital. As this will be the first Kirby recital for some of you, I may as well explain a few things so there will be no misunderstanding later on.

"Do you know why most schools have recitals?" he demanded, ruffing his shaggy white eyebrows at them.

Some of the boys grinned foolishly, but no one spoke up.

"He sure is in one of his thunder and lightning spells," Steppin decided. "I wonder what's causing him to look so strict."

Dad nodded to one of the older pupils.

"How about it, Roddy?"

Roddy hesitated. "I wouldn't know for sure, Dad, but they seem to have recitals so the kids' folks can watch them show off."

"That's right; and now, Roddy, suppose you tell us why I put on a yearly recital?"

"Well, Dad, I recall you saying that you wanted to give us a chance to show whether we were any good or not."

"Right again!" Dad raised his head and regarded them sternly. "The point I aim to make clear right at the start is that this is a professional school. When we give a recital, your folks and your friends won't be the only ones here to see you. There will be professional people here, scouts on the lookout for talent, so maybe when I make up my program, it's how you dance that's going to decide for me whether or not you'll be on it.

"It doesn't matter to me whether you are a star boarder or a free boy or how fancy a costume your father and mother aim to get you or how much they are pining to have you appear. So don't bother me about all that. Do I make myself clear?"

"Yes, sir," the boys replied in chorus.

"The next thing I want to explain is how I set up the program," Dad went on. "On the bulletin board, you'll see a list of the fifteen dance routines I've picked to use for the recital. You boys are free to sign up for any of them you think you can do. Three weeks before the recital I'll give you all a tryout. But remember, there are sixty boys and girls in this school, and only fifteen are going to appear on the program. So if you want to be chosen, you'd better get busy. And now unless you want to ask questions, I've said my say and you're dismissed."

As Dad hobbled back to his rocking chair, the boys stampeded to the bulletin board to study the list of dances Dad had posted. Steppin read down the list until he came to number five, a tap and acrobatic routine. As soon as he could get near enough, he signed his name under it.

Pete was waiting on the high stoop for him when he came out. "Don't you aim to try out for the recital, Pete?" he asked as they sauntered along the snow-covered street.

"No, I'm not good enough yet. I wouldn't have a chance," Pete explained cheerfully. "What did you sign for?"

"That tap and acrobatic routine we just learned."

"Steppin, that's one of the hardest!"

"I know," Steppin nodded. "Pete, I've just got to appear on the recital, and that's the one dance I yearn to do."

"Well, I'd say you've got a fair to middling chance," Pete comforted him. "I don't know anyone that has a much better chance unless maybe it's Roddy. He's good, too."

"Roddy is the best of the lot, the way I figure," Steppin agreed. "He put his name down for that merry-go-round waltz tap as his first choice. So that gives me more of a chance at the other. Look, Pete, will you come over right after supper and play for me so I can practice?"

"Sure," Pete promised. "I'll play for you anytime you say from now 'til the tryout—there's the red light—so long," he shouted back as he dashed across the street.

"So long." Steppin quickened his steps and, without thinking, his feet began trying out the first steps of the tap and acrobatic routine. Brush and tap, and tap, tap, tap, and slide and turn, and over two, three and over two, three. On each "over two, three," Steppin threw himself into a cartwheel, almost colliding with a portly gentleman who was walking his dog.

"Such goings on," the old man muttered indignantly, but Steppin was already out of earshot.

He heard the familiar sound of piano scales as he ran down their basement steps.

"Mary Ellis is sure sticking to her promise about practicing," he thought.

"Hurry up and come out to the kitchen as soon as you are finished," he shouted when Mary Ellis had let him in. "I've got some important news."

"I'm all finished," Mary Ellis explained. "I was just doing a little extra practice until it's time to set the table."

"Come on then," Steppin led the way. "I want to tell Mom, too."

"Steppin, something just tells me you will be chosen for sure," Mary Ellis assured him loyally when he told them about the recital.

"I wish something would tell me for sure," Steppin confessed.

"Well, time will tell," Mrs. Stebbins said complacently. "You can only do your best and harbor no regrets."

Later, when Pete and Snakey and Virginia came, they cleared the center of the parlor and rolled up the grass run. Pete played the piano while Steppin went through the routine.

"That looks great," Snakey told him. "All I've got to say is if any boy says he can do it better, he's got to show me."

"I think I could do it even faster if I had more room," Steppin said. "How does it look to you, Pete?"

Pete was sitting with his chin in his hands in what Steppin called one of his pondering spells.

"You know, Steppin, I've just been thinking. Every boy or girl who tries out for that routine will do it as fast and furious as he can. I've got a hunch you'll stand a better chance if you do something different."

"How do you mean 'different,' Pete?"

"I mean do it slow and easy. You could keep your steps neat and snappy, of course, but you'd make it look lazy and aimless as if you were dancing just because you happened to feel like dancing. Listen, while I give you an idea of what I mean."

Pete swung around to the keyboard and played a few measures of a droll melody.

Steppin listened intently, his black eyes gleaming. "Say, Pete, play that again, will you?" As Pete obligingly repeated the music, Steppin softly tapped out the first steps of the dance.

"Boy," he exclaimed. "Pete, I think we've got something for sure."

"Why, that's a beautiful piece," Mary Ellis exclaimed. "What is the name of it, Pete?"

"It's called 'The Funeral March of a Marionette.'"

"It's a right cheerful funeral," Steppin said. "And like you say, Pete, it's soft and easy, but it has a lot of snap, too."

"I was sure you'd like the idea," Pete beamed. "What would you say to working out the whole dance in a kind of slow motion and calling it 'The Lazy Acrobat'?"

Steppin poised himself eagerly. "Come on, let's try it."

When ten o'clock came, Pete and Steppin had the dance routine worked out to the new music.

"Now, all I have to do is practice my feet off from now to the tryout," Steppin sighed. "It's going to be hard, of course, because it's a heap easier to do cartwheels and backflips fast. But it sure will be different. And for better or worse, it's going to be my dance."

"We have a phonograph record of the funeral march," Pete told Steppin. "I'll bring it to the studio tomorrow so you can practice there. Then, at night, I'll play for you here."

"Mom," Steppin pleaded, "couldn't we go through it just once more?"

"No, Steppin. I know too well what it means to be kept awake by noise all hours of the night. I can't expect the tenants to quiet down at ten o'clock unless we do, too. You two have done enough for one night anyway. It's time to have some cocoa and cake and call it a night."

During the days that followed, Steppin got to know the music of "The Funeral March of a Marionette" as well as he knew his own name. Whatever he was doing, the plaintive, sprightly melody ran through his head.

"When I'm riding on the bus, I hear the wheels playing

it, and I wriggle my toes to keep the time; when I walk, I'm counting out my steps to it, and in school, I say multiplication tables to it," he complained. "Next thing I know, I'll be saying my prayers to the tune of that piece."

He had never in his life stuck to anything as faithfully as he did to his practice for the tryout. Sometimes he thought that the dance was working out beautifully, and at these times he longed for the day of the tryout to come. At other times, he was sure that the music was dull and the dance was slow and uninteresting, and then he was full of doubts about his chances of being chosen.

One bleak, gloomy afternoon, Steppin was practicing the dance at the studio. He always chose a time when he was sure he would be alone, as he did not want any of the other boys to see his dance before the tryout. He had put a fresh needle in the phonograph and was going through the routine for the last time when he caught a glimpse of a man reflected in the mirror. He whirled around to the door, and his face broke out in a broad grin when he saw that the intruder was Bob Williams.

"I thought you were still on the road," he blurted out.

"So I was," Bob smiled. "I just got in. What have you got there, Steppin?"

"You mean this dance I'm hacking away at?" Steppin, remembering the last time Bob had seen him dance, stuttered with embarrassment. "Why, it's just something I'm fooling around with. I thought maybe I'd use it at the tryout for the recital."

Bob went over to the phonograph and moved the needle back to the beginning of the record.

"Go on—let's see it."

Steppin obediently caught step and started in.

"Whether he likes it or not, it won't be so bad this time," he thought. "'Cause now, I know I'm not so hot of a dancer."

Bob leaned easily against the phonograph cabinet and watched Steppin.

"That's not bad," he commented when the dance was finished. "Not bad at all!"

"Do you think maybe Dad will like it?" Steppin asked eagerly.

"It's hard to say," Bob reflected. "But I wouldn't be at all surprised if he might. It's quite a little novelty number, Steppin."

Steppin felt a happy glow spread from the tips of his toes to the top of his curly black head.

"Would you mind giving me a few pointers?" he stammered eagerly. "I'd sure appreciate it if you would."

Bob stroked his chin gravely as he considered the matter.

"Your main fault as I see it is that your taps are pretty noisy. Why do you work so hard at it, Steppin?"

"Well, you see, Mr. Williams, when I'm doing the dance so slowly, I'm afraid I'll mush it and my feet won't talk loud enough."

Bob shook his head, laughing.

"Don't try to make your feet shout, Steppin, make them whisper. Look!"

Bob's feet tapped out some steps as lightly and easily as if his body was suspended from the ceiling on wires, but every tap was as clear and distinct as a pistol shot.

"I get you," Steppin beamed. "You make your feet whisper, but they whisper out loud. I'll surely keep that in mind."

"That's the idea," Bob nodded.

Steppin took the record off the phonograph and slid it under a pile of records in the cabinet.

"I'll clear out now, Mr. Williams, so you can get to work. So long and thanks a heap."

"Good luck at the tryout!" Bob called after him.

His chance meeting with Bob Williams did much to reassure Steppin during the few days that remained before the tryout.

"If Bob likes my dance, it's bound to be good," he comforted himself whenever his old doubts returned.

Whenever he was practicing, he tried to keep Bob's suggestions in mind.

"Don't shout your taps, make them whisper out loud," he charged himself, and he strove to achieve the incredible ease and lightness that had earned for Bob his reputation as the world's greatest tap dancer.

"You know, Steppin, your dance looks better and better," Pete told him. "I don't know how to explain it, but your taps sound louder but softer all at the same time."

Steppin was delighted that Pete had noticed the improvement. "I know what you mean, Pete, and that's exactly the way I'm trying to make them sound!"

Steppin didn't know whether he was glad or sorry when the day of the tryout finally came. It would be a relief to have the long suspense over at last, but then, too, it might mean the end of all his hopes. As he wandered nervously among the crowd of boys and girls gathered in the studio, he wavered between joy and despair.

He had never seen so many of the boys and girls together before, and certainly they had never been so quiet. The very room seemed hushed and edgy. Just before they began, Steppin was surprised to see a strange white man walk in and sit down beside Dad. Roddy Bates told him that it was Art Graves, a real Broadway stage director, and that he always helped Dad direct his recitals.

Steppin was one of three who had chosen the tap and acrobatic routine and the last to dance it at the tryout. While each of the other two boys went through with it, Steppin studied them critically, trying to compare his performance with theirs. As Pete had predicted, the boys danced as fast and energetically as they could. Both were good dancers and, although Dad and Mr. Graves made no comment, the children heartily applauded each of them.

"Maybe I should have worked it up faster, after all," Steppin worried. "Well, even so, it's too late now, so I'll just have to put it over the best way I know how."

While Pete played the soft prelude, Steppin shuffled aimlessly out on the floor. With his hands in his pockets and his head hunched forward, he began a slow syncopated walk while his toes flipped imaginary trifles from his path. Then, when the first movement began with no apparent change of tempo, Steppin began to tap.

His entire routine was built on the theme of an indolent dancer. Whenever he turned a cartwheel, he raised his arms, stretched his mouth in an enormous yawn and then slowly but with perfect control and timing, threw himself head over heels. When he bent backwards to the floor, he doubled over as limply as if he had no bones to hold him up, and when he did a split, he let his face drop against his forward knee so that for a few seconds it seemed as if he had decided not to finish the dance at all. For his final step, he gave a terrific yawn and fell limply forward. As his hands touched the floor, he let his feet slide slowly out from under him. While Pete played the finale, Steppin lay with one hand under his cheek, sprawled on the floor, snoring.

He was completely surprised at the enthusiastic clapping and stamping that greeted him as he scrambled to his feet.

"Good for you, Steppin! —Say, Step, that was great," he heard on all sides as he hurried to his seat.

"The kids liked it," he exulted, and unconsciously his eyes sought Dad's corner.

Dad and Mr. Graves had their heads together, talking, and Dad was smiling and nodding, but Steppin knew no word would be spoken until everyone had danced. Suddenly he realized that he couldn't stay and endure the suspense any longer. He nudged Pete, who had sat down beside him.

"Look, Pete, I can't take it. I've got to get out of here," he whispered. "I'll wait at the Greek's. As soon as you know who Dad chooses, you come and tell me."

In the quiet back room of the Greek ice cream parlor, Steppin sat and worried. When his order, a double chocolate

Mexican soda, was set before him, he absently traced designs with his straw in the froth as if he didn't know it was his favorite treat. He tried to keep from looking at the clock on the wall, for he was sure the hands moved even more slowly when he watched them.

Fifteen minutes dragged by. Would Pete never come? Maybe Dad had decided against him, and Pete hadn't the heart to break the news. "But that wasn't like Pete," Steppin remembered. "If Pete made a promise, he'd keep it, no matter what happened."

He decided to drink his soda very slowly without once looking at the clock. Surely by that time, Pete would be there with some news.

"It must have taken me ten minutes at the very least," Steppin thought as he moved the straw about and sucked up every last bit of froth from the glass. "Pete's bound to come now."

But when he looked up, he found that it had taken him less than five minutes, and Pete was not in sight.

He started counting slowly to a hundred, but halfway through he lost count and began thinking how awful he would feel when Pete came and told him he had failed.

"I'll try to take it like a man," he decided. "But there's no use of me pretending I don't care because Pete knows I care a heap. Poor Pete will feel almost as sunk as I do."

"It's all right, Pete," he muttered to himself. "I tried my best, but it just wasn't in the cards."

Steppin threw back his shoulders and raised his empty glass dramatically. "Well, better luck next time!"

"Steppin, Steppin!—"

Steppin choked back a sob of self-pity as he heard Pete shouting from the doorway.

"You should have stayed, Step," Pete panted as he raced through the store. "They clapped and yelled all over again when Dad announced you had won your place on the recital. I knew you'd be chosen," he sighed as he slid into his chair.

"What's the matter?" Pete demanded. "Why don't you say how tickled you are or something—hey, Joe, will you please bring me a banana split?" he called out to the soda clerk.

Steppin relaxed, and his face expanded in a blissful smile. "Make it two, Joe!" he bellowed.

During the next two weeks, Steppin lived in a rosy world of his own. Whether he was home or at school, his thoughts were always on his coming appearance at the recital. He was happily unaware that Miss Dalton, his teacher, was thoroughly exasperated with him, and that even his mother's patience was almost exhausted. The only thing that mattered to Steppin was the daily rehearsal at the studio.

Promptly at four-thirty, Mr. Graves would settle his great bulk comfortably in an armchair and the rehearsal would begin. Working with a professional director like Mr. Graves was a wonderful experience. He seemed to know just how to bring out the best in every one of them as, day after day, he coached them in their dances. Always patient, always smiling, he encouraged the timid with kind words and mildly rebuked those who were inclined to be too cocky. Steppin knew that all of them were dancing even better than they had at the tryout.

The last two rehearsals were held in the Renaissance, the huge hall that Dad had rented for the recital. Here, with a real stage, curtains, footlights, and a three-piece orchestra to play for them, Steppin felt that at last his dream of becoming a professional dancer was coming true.

Mr. Graves insisted upon having every detail of the performance carried out in the most professional manner. He taught them just how to come out from the wings, how to make an exit, and how to take a curtain call. Nothing was left to chance, and even the dress rehearsal on the afternoon before the recital went off without any serious mistakes. Steppin never felt calmer and more self-possessed than he did on this last afternoon.

He had gained so much confidence that he felt sure his fear of facing an audience was gone forever. After the rehearsal he went home and ate a light supper, as Mr. Graves had advised. Then while his mother and Mary Ellis marveled at his composure, he carefully dressed himself for the evening performance.

At seven o'clock he returned to the Renaissance. As soon as he saw the other boys and girls waiting backstage, he knew that every one of them was suffering from stage fright. Before many minutes, much to his surprise, Steppin began to feel as tense and nervous as ever.

"Even Roddy looks scared out of his wits," Steppin thought as he watched the school's star performer pacing nervously back and forth and mopping his brown face with his spotless handkerchief.

Only Dad and Mr. Graves were in good spirits. They were as cheerful and reassuring as if they knew beforehand that the recital was going to be a success.

Promptly at fifteen minutes after eight, the orchestra played a short overture while Ravella Dixon, who was first on the program, stood waiting in the wings. Ravella had been sniffling and wiping her eyes every few minutes ever since she arrived.

"Will she get up enough nerve to go on?" Steppin's own heart began thumping louder and louder as he watched Ravella's trembling fingers, smoothing the billowing flounces of her bright blue-and-silver costume.

Ravella had made her entrance and was halfway through her dance before Steppin relaxed enough to take a breath.

"Ravella is all right!" he thought. "A few minutes ago she was crying like a baby, and here she is dancing away and smiling as if she liked it. I only hope I'll do as well."

"How are you, Steppin?" Steppin jerked his eyes from the stage. He even managed to produce a sickly smile when he discovered Bob Williams grinning down at him.

"I'm scared out of my skin almost," Steppin confessed. "Mr.

Williams, do you reckon I'll always be smote like this when I have to dance in public? Seems like I ought to get used to it by and by."

"I'll tell you a secret, Steppin." Bob leaned over and whispered in his ear. "I'm always scared, too!"

Steppin exclaimed, "Ah, but you're just kidding me."

"No, sir, I was never more serious in my life," Bob insisted. "I'm always as jittery as a cat before I go on. Most everyone is, Steppin. But that scared feeling does something for you. It winds you up inside and puts you on your toes. Then when you really begin to dance, it makes you do your best. That's the reason a performance before an audience is always better than any rehearsal."

"If being scared of an audience is going to make me dance better, you'll sure have a rival when I get through," Steppin told him.

"That's the spirit!" Bob chuckled. "Walk right out there and knock them cold."

"I'll try my best," Steppin promised as Bob strolled over to speak to another worried youngster.

Steppin felt better after his talk with Bob. Even when he was standing in the wings, waiting for his cue, he was not as frightened as he had been earlier in the evening.

"Feeling scared isn't anything to worry about," he whispered to himself. "Even Bob Williams is scared, and just look how he puts over a dance."

And once he actually began to dance, he realized that Bob was right in what he had said about performing before an audience. In spite of his first panic, when he saw the sea of shadowy faces before him, he knew even before he had finished that he had never danced better in his life.

"That was nice work, Steppin." Dad thumped him on the back affectionately and rumpled his neat hair as he returned backstage after his third curtain call.

"What did I tell you, Steppin?" Bob Williams grinned.

"You told me plenty, and I'm surely much obliged to you," Steppin said as they shook hands. "Now, I know I'll always be scared before an audience, but what's more, I know I'll always be able to go through with it."

Steppin sat down on the floor with the young dancers who had already appeared and were now enjoying the rest of the recital. They watched each dance as intently as if they were seeing it for the first time and whispered their compliments to the performer as he or she finished and joined them.

The last number on the program was always given to the best dancer in the school. This honor had been given to Roddy. As Dad firmly believed in quality rather than quantity in his dance recitals, they were never very long. At twenty minutes after nine, the orchestra was playing the prelude of the lilting waltz music of Roddy's Merry-go-Round tap dance. Roddy had a real gift for dancing, and he was one of the hardest workers in the school. Everyone knew he would do well as he always did, but even his friends backstage were impressed by the ease and grace with which he executed the intricate steps of the Merry-go-Round, which was considered the most advanced and difficult of all Dad's dance routines.

Steppin stood up so that he could follow more closely the pattern of Roddy's nimble feet.

"Roddy is good, no fooling," he thought. "I don't see how even a professional could do much better."

When Roddy slid lightly and effortlessly into the final and most difficult step and began whirling and tapping on one foot, Steppin completely forgot Mr. Graves' order "Not a sound from backstage" and began clapping his hands as hard as he could. He was relieved when he realized that everyone—Mr. Graves, Bob, and even Dad himself—were applauding Roddy as he bowed and skipped back to join them.

Bob was standing beside Steppin.

"That, Steppin, my boy, is what I call dancing," he beamed as

Roddy went out again and again in response to the clapping and cries for an encore from the audience.

Steppin nodded gravely. "I was just thinking not many professionals could do any better. Maybe not any except you."

Bob smiled broadly.

"No, Steppin, there are plenty of professionals that could do it just as well, but there is only one that ever did it any better, and that is the man who invented it—Dad Kirby."

"Dad!" Steppin couldn't conceal his surprise, and he glanced over at Dad, who was leaning lightly on his crutch, talking to a strange man who had been backstage all evening.

"That's right, Steppin." Bob, too, glanced at Dad, a world of affection and admiration lighting up his handsome brown face. "Dad Kirby was the greatest of them all until he got cracked up in the war, and don't ever let anyone tell you anything different, Steppin. Most men would have given up when they found their career was ruined, but not Dad. He just picked up the pieces and started all over again. And because he's just naturally bound to put his whole heart and soul into anything he takes on, you kids have the best teacher in the world."

Steppin was just going to agree with all his heart when Dad Kirby tapped his cane for attention. Everyone stopped talking and looked toward him. He and the blond stranger and Roddy were standing together. Roddy's face wore a smile that spread from ear to ear, and his even, white teeth gleamed like a double row of piano keys.

"Boys and girls, I want you to meet my good friend Jack Cunningham, who has done us a real favor by coming to the recital tonight," announced Dad, nodding his head toward the stranger. "Jack has a few words to say to you."

"Boys and girls, I just want to tell you that I've really enjoyed watching your recital. You all did very well, and you're a real credit to the school and to Mr. Kirby. The only one I've got any complaint against is this Bates fellow." Mr. Cunningham jerked his head toward Roddy, who grinned broader than ever.

"Now, I don't want you to misunderstand me," resumed Mr. Cunningham. "I'm not saying Roddy Bates isn't good. To tell the truth, I think he's a little too good, and if Dad kept him on here, he might begin to get uppity. So, I'm sure you'll all be pleased to hear I've decided to hire him for a new all-colored revue that's going to start rehearsals in a few weeks. And you might be interested to know he is going to appear in a number with another dancer who is with us this evening and who is to be a star in the revue." Mr. Cunningham bowed at Bob Williams. "The one and only Bob Williams!"

"Hurrah!" exulted Steppin as he roared and clapped his hands until his palms were numb. "It was hard work that got Roddy his big chance. I don't know anyone I'd rather see get a break than Roddy."

"For he's a jolly good fellow"—Steppin broke off his musings and loudly chimed in with the chorus of lusty young voices that roared their good will and good wishes to Roddy Bates.

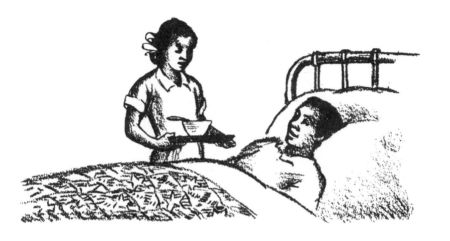

CHAPTER 13

Hard Times Come Knocking

For the first few weeks after the recital, life seemed very dull to Steppin. It was hard to settle down to humdrum, everyday things again with no tryout and no recital to dream about. School seemed more tedious than ever as he had had to work twice as hard to make up for his lack of effort during rehearsals. He had had midterm examinations to worry about, too, for Steppin knew if he failed in any of his subjects, his mother would insist upon his spending less time dancing.

On the Thursday before Easter, he was relieved when he was given his report card and learned that he had been promoted.

"All my old exams are over, and now I've got over a week of vacation to cheer me, and sooner or later summer vacation is bound to come, so things might be worse," Steppin told himself as he hurried home.

He burst into the kitchen and tossed his cap and his strap of despised homework books on a chair before he saw Miss Walker, the Henry Street Visiting Nurse, washing her hands at the kitchen sink. Her little black bag was propped open on the kitchen table, and beside it, on a paper napkin, Steppin saw a fever thermometer and the various little bottles she always took out when she came to visit them.

"How do you do, Steppin? I was hoping you would come in before I left," Miss Walker greeted him.

"How do you do? Is Mary Ellis sick, Miss Walker?" asked Steppin all in one breath.

"No, Mary Ellis has gone to the drugstore," Miss Walker explained. "It's your mother I came to see today."

"My mother? Is Mom sick?" Steppin's eyes opened so wide they showed white.

"Is she sick in bed?" he asked, starting impulsively toward her room.

"Wait, Steppin," Miss Walker stopped him. "Your mother is sleeping now. Don't look so frightened. Your mother will be all right soon if she has good care," she reassured him. "That's what I wanted to talk to you about."

Miss Walker had repacked and closed her bag. After she rolled down the sleeves of her pretty blue uniform and snapped on her neat, white cuffs, she sat down at the table. Steppin slid into a chair opposite her.

"Steppin, your mother hasn't been feeling very well for a few weeks, and this morning she went to see Dr. Marker. The doctor found that her heart isn't as strong as it should be, and he says she must rest in bed for at least two weeks. He wanted her to go to the hospital, but she thought she would be happier in her own bed at home. The doctor telephoned our office and asked me to come in and see if your mother had the medicine he ordered and to make sure there would be someone to cook her meals and wait on her."

"Mary Ellis and I will take care of Mom, Miss Walker, just as well as if she was in the hospital," Steppin said. "Mary Ellis is a right good cook, so she can fix up her meals, and I'll wait on her hand and foot and wash dishes and all like that. It's vacation now, anyway, and when school starts I know Mrs. Mack will step in and help, especially as Mom nursed her that time she got took down with a broken arm."

"That's what I told the doctor," Miss Walker smiled. "I said I was sure you two could look after things, and of course I'll come in at least once a day to bathe Mrs. Stebbins and see how you are getting along."

"We will surely be in your favor if you will," said Steppin gratefully. "Only, Miss Walker"—Steppin hesitated, and the worried look came into his eyes again.

"Only what, Steppin?" Miss Walker encouraged him.

"Miss Walker, if Mom rests in bed as long as the doctor says she should and we care for her just like you tell us—will she get all well again?"

Mary Ellis came in just then, and Miss Walker waited until she had tiptoed over and sat down between them.

"That is another thing I wanted to talk about with both of you," Miss Walker told them. "You know, your mother has been working very hard for a long, long time. Now, the doctor says she will have to take things easier, and he thinks working as superintendent of this big house is too much for her. If she does give up this job, I'm wondering if you have any relatives who would help her take care of you?"

"We haven't any kinfolk at all," Mary Ellis told her.

"Maybe the owner of the house would let me be the super," Steppin suggested hopefully. "I know about everything that has to be done, and I'm sure I could do it."

"I'm sure you could, too," agreed Miss Walker. "Only, you know, there are a lot of things a superintendent has to do that the owner might think you were too young to handle—things like dealing with the tenants and collecting the rent and looking after repairs and watching out for fire hazards."

"I reckon you are right," Steppin sighed. "I wish I was bigger for my age. I'd stand a better chance of getting almost any job."

"Me, too," spoke up Mary Ellis. "I'd do anything to help take care of Mom. Oh, why does it take so long for a body to get grown up!"

Mary Ellis turned her head away from them and wiped her sleeve over her eyes.

Miss Walker put her arm around Mary Ellis and smiled at Steppin's woebegone face.

"My goodness, this will never do," she said cheerfully. "After all, we don't have to decide on anything today. I only wanted to talk to you because the doctor doesn't want your mother to be worried about anything. He hasn't said anything to her about giving up her work here, and I was hoping you might have some relative or friend who might help us plan."

"Friend?" Steppin sat up and his face brightened. "I've got a friend, Miss Walker, Bob Williams."

"Do you mean Bob Williams, the dancer?" Miss Walker asked incredulously.

"Sure," Steppin beamed. "He's the very one. He's been a true friend to me for a long time."

"He's been a true friend to all of us," Mary Ellis put in. "Maybe he could help us scheme up some way to take care of Mom."

"Bob Williams has been a good friend to many people here in Harlem," said Miss Walker. "But, Steppin, do you really know him well enough so that you would feel free to ask his advice?"

"I know him even better than I know you, Miss Walker, and I'm asking your advice right now."

Miss Walker laughed. "But giving advice is part of my job, you know, Steppin. Mr. Williams is a very famous man, and I imagine he has a great many people making demands upon his time and asking favors of him. May I ask how you became acquainted with him?"

Steppin and Mary Ellis both started talking at once in their eagerness to tell Miss Walker about the memorable day when Steppin met Bob Williams at the theatre and all the exciting events that had come into their lives since that day. Miss Walker was interested, but their story threatened to be very long, so when she had heard enough to assure herself that Steppin really did know the most famous person in Harlem, she tactfully interrupted them.

"Steppin, I think your idea of talking things over with Bob Williams is an excellent plan. He may not be able to do anything, but two heads are better than one."

"And with you and Steppin and Mr. Williams and me, we will have four heads," Mary Ellis pointed out. "So we surely ought to scheme up something."

"That's right," agreed Miss Walker. "How soon do you suppose you could talk with Mr. Williams, Steppin?"

Steppin considered.

"Well, I know he is rehearsing for a new play, so most likely he won't be working tonight. Maybe I could try to see him right after supper."

"Do you know where he lives?" Miss Walker asked.

"Do I know where Bob Williams lives!" Steppin stared at her in amazement. "Golly, Miss Walker, I would have said there wasn't more than three people in Harlem that didn't know that."

"Oh," Miss Walker said meekly, realizing that she was one of the three ignorant people of whom Steppin spoke with such scorn.

"Mary Ellis," Mrs. Stebbins called from her bedroom.

"There, your mother is calling," Miss Walker said briskly. "I'll go in with you and bid her good afternoon."

"And remember," she charged them, "Not a word to her of what we've been discussing. And you must promise me that you will keep up a cheerful front."

"We will, Miss Walker," Steppin and Mary Ellis promised. They were quite reassured when they saw their mother. Except that for the first time in their lives they found her in bed before nightfall, she looked just the same as always.

"I'm all right," she insisted brightly. "This staying in bed is just something that doctor and Miss Walker cooked up. I reckon they think we are so rich I can afford to take one of those stylish rest cures I've heard about."

"You've earned a rest, and we are going to see that you get it," Miss Walker smiled.

After she had written down and explained everything they were to do, she said "goodbye" and promised them an early visit in the morning.

Mary Ellis cooked supper and set her mother's tray with the best china and linen, and Steppin carried it in to her. As soon as they had finished their own supper, Steppin left Mary Ellis reading the instructions Miss Walker had given them and slipped quietly out of the house.

"Maybe I should have brought an identification or something to help get me in," Steppin worried as he walked into the court of the elegant apartment house in which his hero lived. "A rich man like Bob Williams might have a whole raft of hired help all dolled up in knee britches, with ribbons and lace like pictures on valentines.

"I'll just tell them it's urgent and ask them to tell Mr. Williams who I am," he decided as he rang the bell.

Steppin was quite surprised when Bob Williams himself opened the door.

"Mr. Williams, I'm sorry to make myself a bother like this, but I'm in a fix for sure," Steppin announced.

"That's all right, Steppin. I'm glad to see you, and I'm sorry to hear you are in trouble. Come on in and tell me about it."

Steppin followed Bob Williams into a living room. He was too excited to pay much attention to his surroundings, and afterward, when Mary Ellis begged him for details, he could only remember that the room had shiny, slippery floors and thick, soft rugs, a lot of soft chairs and sofas, and a beautiful grand piano, and that it was without doubt the handsomest room he had ever seen.

As briefly as possible, Steppin explained that his mother

was sick and that she would have to give up her position as superintendent.

"So you see, Mr. Williams, I've just got to find me a job so I can care for her and Mary Ellis," he finished earnestly.

"But, Steppin, you are pretty young to start supporting a family. And then, there's your schooling and your dancing—you wouldn't want to give them up."

"I wouldn't mind about school; to tell the truth, I'd just as lief stop as not, and as for dancing," Steppin sighed and shook his head, "you know, Mr. Williams, if only this morning anyone would have told me I'd even think of giving up dancing, I would have said they were plumb crazy. But now, when I have to choose between dancing and taking care of Mom and getting her well, I see things differently. Even if I never dance another step, I put her first. So you see, I just have to find a job."

Bob smiled understandingly. "Of course I see, Steppin, and I'll try to help you find something. You'd better give me your address, by the way, so I can get in touch with you if I hear of anything. I've got to go out in a few minutes, so I'll run you home. In the meantime, Steppin, you keep a stiff upper lip; and maybe, when you least expect it, good fortune will come your way."

Mary Ellis was in their mother's room when Steppin got home. After she had smoothed her mother's bed and rubbed her back and carefully measured out and given the sleeping medicine the doctor had ordered, she joined Steppin in the kitchen. When Steppin told her about his talk with Bob and his promise to try to help him find a job, she looked more distressed than pleased. "Oh, Steppin, I just can't bear to have you give up your dancing career," she exclaimed. "Especially when you have worked so hard at it and done so well in the recital. There must be some other way. Maybe I could find somebody who would pay me to take care of children or do housework for them."

"No!" Steppin almost shouted, and then, as Mary Ellis cautioned him, he lowered his voice. "Mary Ellis, the women folk have been taking care of this family long enough. I'm the man of the family, and it's my place to do it; and some way or other, I'm bound I will."

Mary Ellis laid her small brown hand over Steppin's. "I just know you will find a way to care for Mom, Steppin," she declared. "Only I'm going to keep hoping and praying with all my might and main that you will find a way to keep on with your dancing, too."

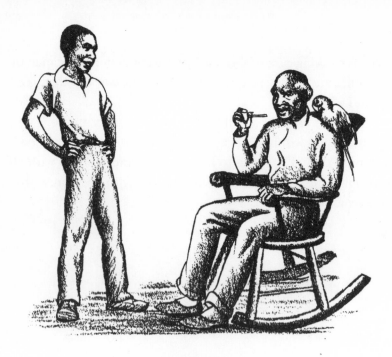

CHAPTER 14

Bob Williams
Keeps His Word

"I always knew there was a heap of kindness in the world, and it only takes a touch of trouble to bring it to full flower," Mrs. Stebbins remarked to Mary Ellis one Saturday morning. "Everybody has been so kind that keeping in bed has been more of a pleasure than a trial. If it keeps on and you and Miss Walker continue to pamper me as you have, I won't want to get up even when the doctor says I may."

"People surely have been kind," agreed Mary Ellis, "but then you have been doing for others all your life, and now your good deeds are coming back to you."

"'Cast thy bread upon the waters,'" Mrs. Stebbins softly quoted.

"And after many days, it will return to you buttered an inch thick," affirmed Mary Ellis. "You helped Mrs. Mack when she broke her arm, and now she does all the heavy chores and looks after the tenants. You were always doing something kind for Mr. Kee, and now you'd think we were doing him a favor to let him keep us in fresh linen while you are in bed. And you always worked harder than anyone in the Ladies' Aid, so it's no more than right for them to bring you plenty of good things to eat."

Mrs. Stebbins smiled at her eager little daughter. "I think I'm receiving a lot more than I've ever given," she said. "Mrs. Bergeret certainly had no call to do so much, loaning me a radio and making me this lovely bed jacket. And whatever have we done to deserve so much kindness from Miss Walker?"

"Well, if you didn't do anything special for them, you surely did it for someone else—there's Miss Walker now," Mary Ellis broke off as she caught a glimpse of the visiting nurse in her grey coat and hat coming down the basement stairs.

"I have everything ready for you, and I did everything on the list that you left for me," Mary Ellis reported as Miss Walker took off her wraps and opened her bag. "I'll wash my hands, too, and then I'll be ready to help you."

"Mary Ellis, you are a fine little nurse," Miss Walker praised her helper when she had read the neat little chart Mary Ellis had kept and inspected the excellent preparations she had made in her mother's room.

"Yes, Mary Ellis is very handy around a sick room," agreed Mrs. Stebbins. "She has been telling me she thinks she would like to take up nursing when she grows up."

"Would you, Mary Ellis?" Miss Walker asked her.

"I'm sure I'd love it," Mary Ellis declared. "Only Mom has always had her heart set on having me study to be a teacher."

"I haven't set my heart on it, Mary Ellis," her mother assured her. "I suppose it was because I always yearned to be a teacher; I took it for granted that you would want to be one.

"You see, Miss Walker, Mary Ellis has always been so fond of school and studying that I just naturally thought of teaching instead of nursing as her calling."

Miss Walker laughed merrily. "Well, Mrs. Stebbins, being fond of school and studying will never come amiss if she takes up nursing. I started to school when I was six, and counting my three years in training, I've been at it steadily for nearly twenty years. I'm going to college two nights a week right now."

"You don't say!" Mrs. Stebbins marveled. "That just shows how little I know about things. It's not that I don't appreciate nursing, Miss Walker. It's a wonderful work, I know. But I always had the idea nursing was a calling that required clever hands and a kind heart more than book learning."

"A girl with clever hands and a kind heart has a fine start toward being a good nurse, but it takes a lot of hard work and study before she reaches her goal," Miss Walker explained.

"Twenty years seems a powerful long time to go to school," Mary Ellis said. "When will you ever be finished with all your learning, Miss Walker?"

"I'll never finish," Miss Walker told her. "Even if I had learned everything that was known, I couldn't finish because nursing is always growing, and new things are found out. If I stopped studying, I'd soon be out of date. I expect I'll be so old and feeble I'll have to be carried to school in a wheelchair before I stop."

"'It's an ill wind that blows no good,'" Mary Ellis quoted. "And goodness knows, Mom, I'd never want you to get sick just so I could nurse you. But talking with Miss Walker and watching her and learning to help has proved to me that nursing is the call I aim to follow.

"Have you everything you need, Miss Walker?" Mary Ellis

asked. "Because if you have, I thought I'd go to the store while you are here with Mom. Steppin is helping High Pockets in the hall, if you should want him," she added when Miss Walker assured her she could be spared.

"You are looking better every day, Mrs. Stebbins," said Miss Walker.

"I feel as if I could get right up and do a day's work," Mrs. Stebbins replied.

"That will come, too," Miss Walker smiled. "But sickness is always such a problem. I've been wondering if you are getting along all right financially. I hope you don't mind my asking."

"Of course I don't mind, Miss Walker," Mrs. Stebbins said sincerely. "We look upon you as a true friend. So far, everything is all right," she went on to explain. "I have my widow's pension, and that keeps us going. Then as superintendent I get my rent free and ten dollars a month. I don't know how I ever could have managed without my job, but as it is, I've even managed to put a little money in a Postal Savings. I'd always planned to use it to give the children a start toward whatever call they chose to follow. But if I have to use it to carry us until I get back on my feet, I'll be thankful I have it and trust the Lord to help me look after the children's future.

"I've set my heart on having both of them learn a good trade, so they will be able to support themselves. Maybe it's because I've suffered from the lack of having any special training myself that's made me so bent on their having it."

"I think you have done a splendid job," Miss Walker said earnestly. "You make a wonderful home for the children and brought them up to be a real credit to our race. At the office, I'm always talking about Steppin and Mary Ellis, and all the nurses declare you are my pet family."

"They are good children, if I do say so myself," Mrs. Stebbins admitted. "Mary Ellis has been nothing but a joy and a comfort to me since the minute she was born. At heart, Steppin, too, is as good as gold, but there have been times when I couldn't truthfully say he was a comfort."

"They certainly are different," Miss Walker agreed.

"They are as different as day and night," their mother declared. "In some ways, Mary Ellis seems so much steadier. Now, she loves music and she studies at it almost as steady as Steppin does at his dancing. But if Mary Ellis never becomes a great musician, it won't trouble her at all. She will keep right on loving music and taking pleasure in it and be happy and interested in nursing or any other call she follows.

"But Steppin carries all his eggs in one basket. His whole heart and soul are set on becoming a professional dancer. Often I wish he had picked out a more practical goal than dancing, but he is so wrapped up in it that I've never felt I could do anything but encourage him. It worries me, though."

"It worries me, too," Miss Walker thought as she was packing her bag and giving Mary Ellis her instructions. "Poor Steppin's egg basket is a lot nearer toppling over than his mother realizes."

"Any news, Steppin?" she asked as he came quietly into the kitchen.

"No, ma'am, not yet," he told her, "but in this case, I say no news is good news because if Bob Williams hadn't any hopes for me, he would have let me know."

"I only hope and pray Steppin's faith in Bob Williams is justified," Miss Walker thought as she carefully felt her way along the dark hall of the tenement basement.

She knew that Bob Williams' reputation for kindness was as great as his reputation as a dancer. He gave money to every worthy charity in Harlem.

"But it's asking too much to suppose he can be interested in every family in Harlem, too," she argued to herself. "And, anyway, he is only human, and nothing but a miracle will find a worthwhile job that a boy of Steppin's age could fill.

"Well, it takes faith to work miracles, and I've never seen

anyone with greater faith than Steppin has in Bob Williams. I reckon he has plenty for both of us. And in spite of everything, I almost believe some miracle will come to their rescue."

When Miss Walker ran up the steps to the street, she was mildly surprised to see a handsome limousine stop at the curb. When the driver stepped out of the car and asked a group of children on the sidewalk, "Can any of you tell where the Stebbins family lives?" Miss Walker was more than surprised, and her heart skipped a beat.

"This must be no other than Bob Williams," she decided.

"They live in the basement, the last door on the left," she heard herself saying. "I've just come from there."

"Oh, thank you, Nurse." Halfway down the steps the man stopped and looked back. "How is Mrs. Stebbins?" he asked. "Is she well enough to see visitors, I mean?"

"Oh, yes, she is ever so much better." Miss Walker was fairly stammering with excitement.

"That's fine. I hoped I could have a talk with her about something I've got in mind for Steppin. Good morning, Nurse, and thank you."

As Miss Walker hurried along to her next patient, she hummed a happy little tune under her breath.

"I almost feel as if I should beg Steppin's pardon when I think how I mistrusted his faith," she smiled to herself. "Never again will I say I don't believe in miracles when with my own eyes I've seen the biggest man in Harlem go out of his way to keep his promise to a trusting little boy."

Steppin had never doubted for a minute that Bob Williams would remember his promise to help him try to find a job. He hadn't thought much about just how or when Bob would get in touch with him except that he rather expected Bob would send him a letter. When Bob almost bumped into him in the areaway, Steppin was so excited he nearly forgot to ask him in.

"Well, Steppin," said Bob, "I have a line on a job for you. It's going to end your dancing career for a while, so I don't know whether you will be glad or sorry to hear about it."

"I'm sorry about the dancing, but I sure will be grateful for a job," Steppin assured him. "I'm even more set on having a job than I am on dancing, or just as much anyway."

"It isn't any great shakes of a job," Bob told him. "But it's the best I could do on short notice. And if your mother will let you take it, I'm pretty sure the job is yours. I thought it would save time if I talked it over with both of you at once, so if Mrs. Stebbins feels like having a visitor, we can get down to business."

Steppin excused himself and rushed into his mother's room to prepare her for this most important visitor. He noticed with approval how nicely Miss Walker and Mary Ellis had fixed everything. The room was clean and tidy, the bed smooth and spotless, and his mother fresh and dainty in her pretty bed jacket.

"You see, Mrs. Stebbins," Bob began after Steppin introduced them, "Steppin thinks it is about time he began helping you out a little, and I'm inclined to agree with him. He asked me to look around for a job for him, and I've heard of one I think he could fill. They need a boy about his size for the show Roddy and I are rehearsing in—"

"A job in a show!" Steppin interrupted.

"Now don't get all steamed up for nothing," warned Bob. "It's not a big part, and you are not going to do any dancing."

But Steppin couldn't be put down.

"Golly, Mr. Williams, I don't expect a big part, and I know I'm not anywhere near to being a professional dancer. Why, if the job is only scrubbing the theatre or hauling around scenery, I'll be so happy I'll almost bust!"

"Well, well, Steppin, you certainly have changed since that first day I talked to you at Dad's studio," Bob teased.

"I sure have," Steppin agreed ruefully. "You know, Mr. Williams, I still hang my head for shame every time I think how foolish I was then."

Bob threw back his head, laughing. "Steppin, you've come a long way since that day, and I'm glad to say the job is a little better than scrubbing the theatre. It's two small bits in the revue but, of course, it will take as much of your time as if you were carrying the whole show. However, you will be earning more than most boys of your age could ever hope to do, and the experience will be good for you, too."

Bob turned to Mrs. Stebbins. "I'm just assuming Steppin is willing to take the job, so the only thing needed is your consent."

Mrs. Stebbins smiled at Steppin, who looked as happy as any boy could possibly look.

"Mr. Williams, I wouldn't have the heart to stand in Steppin's way, even if I wanted to. The only thing that bothers me is having him miss school. You know, it is hard to go back once you leave and get behind the rest of the class."

"Oh, school doesn't matter, Mom," Steppin said. "It isn't as if I wanted to be a lawyer or a doctor. I know all I'll ever need to know to be a dancer."

"That's what you think," Bob told Steppin. "But whether you need it or not, you've got to go to school until you are seventeen. I was just coming to that, Mrs. Stebbins. He will have to have a tutor for at least two hours a day. There are a lot of things like that to be arranged for him, and since you won't be able to attend to them yourself, I thought I'd have my manager fix him up if it's agreeable to you."

Mrs. Stebbins was not only willing but declared she would consider it a great favor if Mr. Williams could attend to things for her.

Bob rose to leave. "Well, young man," he said to Steppin. "Your next move is to march yourself down to the stage entrance of the Royal at two o'clock sharp this afternoon. Ask for Mr. Cunningham and tell him I sent you. In the meantime, I'll have my manager rush through your working papers so the truant officer won't be after you."

Mary Ellis was almost in tears when she came back from the store and learned she had missed seeing Bob Williams. However, Steppin's joy was so catching that she soon forgot her disappointment and was as excited over his good fortune as he was.

"Isn't it wonderful that we got everything fixed up before Mom even found out she would have to give up her job!" she rejoiced as soon as they were in the kitchen where Mrs. Stebbins could not hear them.

"I'll say," Steppin agreed. "Now if I can make good, and the show turns out all right, she won't have to worry at all."

"I'm sure you will make good, and with Bob Williams in the show, everyone is bound to like it," Mary Ellis said confidently. "Now, I think I'll get our lunch right away, so you will have plenty of time to eat and dress before you go to the theatre."

"I'll help you," Steppin offered.

Mary Ellis shook her head.

"No, Steppin, in the state you are in, I'm afraid you wouldn't be much help. You would most likely put salt in the sugar bowl or dump pepper all over my rice pudding instead of cinnamon."

"Well, if you don't need me, I thought I'd run up to the studio and tell Dad about my job," said Steppin. "I might see some of the fellows there, and I could tell them, too. I just feel as if I'd like to stand on top of a skyscraper and sing out the news to everybody."

"Me, too," Mary Ellis confessed. "I can hardly wait for Miss Walker to come back. Won't her eyes blink open when she hears? And while the soup is heating, I thought I'd step in and tell Mr. Kee and then run up and see Mrs. Mack for a minute, too."

"Maybe we ought to have the news put it up in electric lights, so everyone could see it at once," Steppin suggested, and they both laughed heartily.

At the studio Steppin found Dad sitting in his rocking chair with Minnie perched on his shoulder. When Steppin burst out with his wonderful news, Dad didn't act as pleased as Steppin had anticipated. He took a few puffs on his pipe and didn't say anything.

"Don't you think I can make good, Dad?" Steppin asked anxiously.

Dad turned and gave Steppin one of his rare smiles. "I'm sure you will make good, Steppin," Dad began, and then, "Pipe down, Minnie," he ordered as the parrot started screeching. "Sit down, Son, while I quiet this blasted bird."

Steppin perched himself on the window sill and waited until Dad put Minnie in her cage.

"Sure, you will make good, Steppin, and I'm tickled as can be that you've got a job because I know you need it. Only, I'm bound to say to you the same thing I said to Roddy—'don't let it go to your head.'"

"How do you mean, Dad?"

"I mean just because you are going to get a little taste of professional life, don't get the idea you are all set for life," Dad explained. "I've seen that happen plenty of times. A youngster has a fortunate break and gets a small part in a play and from then on, he thinks he knows it all. Then when the play closes, instead of trying to improve his stuff, he hangs around casting offices looking for another break. He would starve before he would do anything but theatre work, and the only reason he doesn't starve is that he sponges on his friends. Pretty soon his only stage experience is a long way behind him, and people begin talking about him as 'one-dance Roddy' or 'one-play Steppin'!"

"I see what you mean, Dad, and I'll surely heed what you've told me," Steppin said.

"I'm sure you will, and Roddy will, too," Dad replied. "That's why I took the bother to warn you. The both of you have a good start in dancing, and I've been more pleased with you than I ever let on, as I didn't want you to get swelled heads or anything like that."

Steppin had to suppress a chuckle at the idea of anyone in

Dad's school ever getting a swelled head from the miserly praise he handed out.

"The thing is, you can never stop practicing if you want to stay at the top as a dancer," Dad went on. "You can get by for a while when you are young and spry, but if you don't get in the habit of daily practice, old age will creep up on you and settle in your joints, and you will be finished before you know it.

"Now Roddy has come in for an hour's workout and such nearly every day since he joined up with the show, and, if you care to, you are welcome to come with him."

"I'll surely be in your favor if you will let me," Steppin told Dad.

"That's good, and now that I've squashed you down to somewhat near your normal size, let me congratulate you on your job," Dad said.

"I reckon I needed to be squashed down some," Steppin grinned as they shook hands. "It seems like a little success puffs me up like a toy balloon."

CHAPTER 15

Steppin Takes the Helm

Dad's squelching was nothing to what Steppin went through in his new job. Except for Roddy, he was the only one in the cast with no previous stage experience; and even Roddy, who had been rehearsing nearly two weeks, seemed a mountain of wisdom compared to Steppin.

"I never would have believed anyone could be as foolish as I am," Steppin confessed to Roddy after his second rehearsal. "Half of the time I don't know what the director is talking about, and the rest of the time I'm too rattled to do what he says. The things that are torn out of my book would fill fifty dictionaries."

"You catch on after a while," Roddy consoled him. "And Mr. Cunningham isn't half as bad as he lets on. He is a lot like Dad Kirby, and the main thing is don't ever give him any back talk or look uppity. He calls that kind of thing 'temperament,' and it seems that's the one thing he just naturally can't stand. You know that Sidney Ross that is my understudy? Well, one day he started talking back, and his mother began egging him on, and, boy, you should have heard Mr. Cunningham tear into the both of them."

"Sidney is a little baby anyway," Steppin commented. "Imagine having your mother come trailing along, carrying your rubber boots and muffler and all like that.

"'I think you had better put on your sweater, Sidney dear. You are so overheated, and the stage is very draughty.'" Steppin mimicked Mrs. Ross' shrill voice. Roddy laughed.

"She sure does keep him tied by her apron strings. But he is a good dancer and that's the truth," he added. Roddy couldn't bear to have anyone ill-spoken of, even in fun.

As Bob had told him, Steppin's two appearances were only small parts. The first one was in a Harlem street scene, the finale of which was Bob's and Roddy's dance. Steppin's part was that of a street urchin turning a series of lazy cartwheels across the stage and then posing during the dance with the other actors in the scene. His second appearance was in an oriental scene called, "Garden in the Desert," which was the background for one of the show's song hits. All the principal actors and the chorus were to be dressed in extravagant oriental costumes. Steppin himself was to wear a pale-blue satin page-boy costume with a turban of silver cloth topped with rhinestones and blue ostrich plumes. He was to carry an enormous silver tray laden with fruit. Steppin had been fitted for the costume and told about the tray of fruit. So far, however, he had worn his ordinary clothes and carried a battered old tin tray heaped with odds and ends of rubbish from the prop room.

At the first rehearsal, Mr. Cunningham explained his two parts and told him, "For the present, you can just stand in and look pleasant. I'll find some business for you later."

Steppin hadn't the vaguest idea what the director meant, but he soon learned. Mr. Cunningham was forever changing the play, discarding some parts, putting in new ideas, and what he called "business," which meant little things for the various actors to add to their parts. During rehearsals a man sat at a little table and wrote all the changes into the manuscript of the play.

During one of the rehearsals of the desert scene, Steppin was standing in his usual place when the leading lady turned quickly and bumped into him. Steppin tried to look as if nothing unusual had happened.

"Hold it!" the director roared, and Steppin's heart sank, thinking he was about to be a target for one of Mr. Cunningham's sarcastic tirades.

"Steppin, what were you thinking about when Miss Andrews bumped into you just then and you sort of rolled your eyes at her?"

"I didn't know I rolled my eyes," Steppin confessed. "I was just thinking how foolish I was to get in the way, I reckon."

"Well, see if you can do it again, will you?" As Miss Andrews once more turned and bumped into him, Steppin concentrated with all his mind on feeling foolish and rolled his eyes. A ripple of laughter broke out among the people who were sitting in the orchestra.

"You see what I mean?" Mr. Cunningham beamed. "The boy gets an effect there that is bound to be good for a laugh. Be sure you write it in," he warned the patient scriptwriter. "And you, Steppin, see that you don't forget what you are supposed to do," he growled.

Steppin, who was in constant fear of provoking one of Mr. Cunningham's well-known outbursts of temper, hoped with all his heart he would be able to recall his "business" when the time came.

Mr. Cunningham ruled the rehearsals, and his word was law. There was no doubt about that. With the single exception of Bob Williams, whom even Mr. Cunningham seemed to look up to, no one from the leading lady down to the lowliest stagehand was safe from his sharp tongue. By following Roddy's advice to keep out from underfoot when he wasn't needed and to be right on the spot when he was called, Steppin managed to avoid any serious fall from grace for nearly two weeks. But finally his turn came, too.

It was late one afternoon, and Mr. Cunningham for the third time had announced:

"Now we will go through from the beginning once more. This will be the last time for today."

Everything went along as usual until they got to the Harlem street scene which ended with Bob's and Roddy's dance. When the cast was gathered on the scene, Mr. Cunningham called,

"Oh, Boss, you and Roddy may as well go, and I'll have your understudies stand in for you."

Danny Green, the young man who understudied the famous Bob Williams, appeared with alacrity, but although Mr. Cunningham roared "Sidney" half a dozen times, neither Sidney nor his mother could be found.

Everyone was watching Mr. Cunningham. His face was purple with rage, and he rumpled his red hair until it stood up like a brush.

"Where is that kid, anyway?" he bellowed. "Why does his mother think we pay him a salary, anyway?

"Oh, why do playwrights have to put juveniles in shows, and if they must, why, in the name of heaven, can't the kids be born orphans?" Mr. Cunningham wanted to know, but no one ventured to answer him.

Just then Mrs. Ross came tripping in with Sidney in tow. "We just slipped out for a chocolate malt," she explained brightly. "I thought Sidney was looking a little gone, and I was feeling a bit weak myself."

Everybody was braced for another outburst, but after a tense moment in which Mr. Cunningham seemed to be undergoing a heroic effort at self-control, he said:

"All right, we'll pick up with the dance." Steppin never tired of watching Bob and Roddy dance. As Bob danced, Roddy, dressed as an exact miniature of Bob, went through the identical steps behind him. Their pantomime suggested that Bob was not quite sure whether or not Roddy was mimicking him, and there were sudden breaks in the music in which Bob turned quickly as if to try to catch Roddy in the act. On these breaks, Roddy's part was to stop motionless in whatever attitude he was caught and to look innocent and disinterested.

Steppin usually enjoyed watching the understudies dancing almost as well as Bob and Roddy. But this afternoon the rehearsal had been unusually long, and he was tired. As he knew every step of the dance and, at the studio, had gone through it many times with Roddy, he could easily keep track of what was going on by listening to the familiar taps. So halfway through the dance, he began daydreaming.

"Hold it," he heard Mr. Cunningham shout, and then he discovered to his dismay that he was the cause of the delay.

"Where in blazes do you think you are, Steppin?" Mr. Cunningham thundered at him. "If you are half as far away as you look, no one could reach you with a penny postcard. Do you think people are going to pay good money to come here to watch you daydream? Now, get that blank look off your face and for heaven's sake, try to look half as intelligent as a trained poodle—"

Steppin knew only too well what Mr. Cunningham meant. He had heard him scold various members of the cast, and particularly the boys and girls in the chorus, for what he called "letting their faces drag."

"Golly, how did I ever happen to let myself go woolgathering like that?" Steppin groaned as he watched the dance with what he hoped was at least the intelligence of a French poodle.

"I wonder if I'm doing all right now," he worried. "Maybe if I try some of that business Mr. Cunningham taught me in the other scene, I'll look better."

Almost unconsciously, Steppin let his face fall into the droll lines and his eyes roll as he did in the desert garden scene. He heard someone in the pit titter, and then Mrs. Ross' voice shrilled above the piano chords and the tapping feet of the dancers.

"Mr. Cunningham, that Stebbins boy is trying to steal Sidney's act, and I just won't stand it, I tell you."

Sidney glanced behind him to see what Steppin was doing and lost the step. The pianist muttered something and banged an angry chord on the piano. Mrs. Ross continued to splutter indignantly while a murmur of protest rose from the cast.

"Oh, cut it out, Mrs. Ross," someone yelled.

Mr. Cunningham ran up to the stage and shouted, "Silence!"

"Mrs. Ross, what do you mean by breaking in on a rehearsal like this?" he demanded angrily.

Mrs. Ross' voice rose to a hysterical squeal. "I tell you that Stebbins boy was trying to steal Sidney's act. I saw him with my own eyes, and I don't care what you say—I won't stand it."

Mr. Cunningham stared at her for a full minute. When he spoke, his voice was soft as silk which, as everyone knew, was always a bad sign.

"My dear Mrs. Ross," he purred. "I don't see how anyone could steal Sidney's act because in the first place, he hasn't any act.

"I may be wrong, but it was my impression that your darling Sidney was an understudy to Roddy Bates, and that at present he was acting as a stand-in, in, without exception, the worst rehearsal I've ever had the misfortune to conduct."

"Maybe Sidney is an understudy, but he is every bit as good as that Bates boy," Mrs. Ross snapped. "You pick on Sidney, I declare you do."

"Oh, for goodness sakes, Mother," Sidney protested as Mrs. Ross began sniffling and wiping her eyes.

Mr. Cunningham silenced Sidney with one awful look. "I don't pick on anyone, Mrs. Ross," he continued, "and I'll even grant you that Sidney has talent. But I assure you that if his father hadn't been one of my best friends and one of the world's finest, I'd never put up with what I've gone through with you.

"And you there, Stebbins—what's got into you anyway? You sure show signs of developing temperament. You're too young to start anything like that, and if you're figuring on playing along with me, you had better nip it in the bud because if there is one thing I can't stand, it's that."

He stopped abruptly and glanced at his watch. "That's all for today," he announced. "Be here at two o'clock tomorrow, and be here on time."

Steppin lagged behind as the others dashed off joyously. In a way, he was glad Roddy and Bob Williams had left before disgrace overtook him, but then again, he rather hoped they were there so he could talk things over. When he got his coat and hat, something prompted him to look back at the stage before he left. Mr. Cunningham was sitting on a kitchen chair before a table, making notes on a manuscript. Without having any clear idea of what he intended to do or say, Steppin walked over and stood, waiting to catch Mr. Cunningham's eye.

"Well, what do you want?" Mr. Cunningham glowered when he caught sight of him.

"I only wanted to say, sir, that I don't know just what I did back there when Sidney and Mr. Green were dancing, but I reckon I did something terrible, and whatever it was, I won't do it again."

Mr. Cunningham looked at Steppin curiously.

"Say that again, will you?" he asked.

Steppin obediently repeated what he had just said.

"What do you mean, you don't know what you did?" demanded Mr. Cunningham. "What did you think you were doing?"

Steppin explained how he had been pondering on how he could keep from looking blank and how he happened to remember the pantomime he had learned for the other scene.

"I just did it without thinking," he said, "but I didn't aim to cause any trouble or try to make Mrs. Ross mad."

"I believe you, Steppin," Mr. Cunningham said kindly. "I forget sometimes how new you are at this business. As far as Mrs. Ross is concerned, you needn't give it a thought. She—" Mr. Cunningham looked as if he was about to go off on a tirade but thought better of it.

"The thing is, Steppin, since the matter has come up, I'd better take time out and explain what stealing an act or hugging the limelight means so you will never even look guilty of doing it again. Because, Steppin, it's about the lowest thing an actor can do. You see, Son, a revue or a play may have a lot of people in it, but it's nearly always built around a few big names. Take this revue, for example. While people are here, they will enjoy the big chorus and the pretty costumes and all the little bits that make up the show. But next day, or even that night, if someone asks them where they have been, they will say, 'I've been to see *Cafe au Lait,* Bob Williams and Marcia Andrews' show.' And even ten years from now, if anyone mentions the show, Bob and Marcia are the ones they will recall. So the job of the rest of the cast is to do everything in their power to support the stars, since whether the show stands or falls depends on them.

"When a fine song or dance solo is being put over, the one thing in the world that can ruin it is distracting the attention of the audience from the performer. But some actors can't resist attracting attention to themselves, even if it means losing their own bread and butter, and that's what we mean by trying to steal the limelight.

"When I told you to lift your face, Steppin, I meant just that. You should watch the dance as if you were pleased and interested, and that helps to keep the audience watching it, too."

A light suddenly dawned for Steppin. "You mean I should look interested like Bob Williams does when his pianist is playing a piano solo?"

"That's exactly what I mean," Mr. Cunningham nodded, "and if there are any other points of stage etiquette you're in doubt about, you can safely take Bob for a guide. If all actors were like him, a show could just about run without a director. But that's always the way—the better they are, the easier they are to handle. Boy and man, I've seen plenty of them, and I've never met any better than Bob.

"Jumping catfish—look at the time!" Mr. Cunningham shouted. "You clear out of here or the next thing I know I'll have the whole Children's Aid Society jumping on me for working you overtime, to say nothing of having your mother down here, making scenes at rehearsals."

Steppin had to laugh at the idea of his quiet, dignified mother ever carrying on and making a scene at a rehearsal.

"Whatever trouble I get into, it surely won't be her fault," he thought.

"There's no use crying over spilt milk, and what is done, is done, but I sure will watch my step from now on; and if I do anything that even looks like stealing an act again, it will be because I'm plumb out of my head," he promised himself.

CHAPTER 16

Steppin Stebbins, Dancer

As Roddy had predicted, Steppin soon caught on to the ways of the theatre. What with daily rehearsals and his school work with the tutor, he had almost no time to himself and, except when he went to Dad's studio for his morning practice, he seldom saw any of his old friends. Mr. Cunningham still raged and blustered, and Steppin came in for his share of the director's sarcasm. But in spite of everything, he was perfectly contented with his new life, and the day that he took his first paycheck home to his mother was the proudest he had ever known.

When the date of the play's opening night was announced, a

frenzy of excitement swept over the cast. Everyone started wondering whether the play would open in New York or whether it would be taken to some smaller city for a tryout. At the next to the last rehearsal, they were told that, come what may, the show would open in New York.

The final rehearsal on the afternoon before the first performance was a nightmare to all of them. Everything seemed to go wrong. Actors missed their cues and forgot their lines, and dancers forgot their steps. Even the technicians lost their skill and turned the spotlights on the empty stage instead of on the stars. Mr. Cunningham worked himself into such a rage that Steppin wouldn't have been at all surprised if he had closed the show right then and there.

At the rate things were going, Steppin expected Mr. Cunningham would make them go right on rehearsing until it was time for the evening performance to begin. He could hardly believe his ears when, long before the usual time, the director shouted his ever-welcome, "That's all for today."

Mrs. Stebbins was almost well now and was sitting in an armchair by the kitchen window when Steppin came in. Mary Ellis was bustling about, setting the table and cooking their lunch. As usual, they were bubbling over with questions about the rehearsal. At first Steppin could hardly bear to talk about it, but finally he broke down and told them about the terrible morning they had had and all the mistakes that had been made.

"For the very first time, I'm troubled for fear the show won't be a success," he confessed.

"I don't know anything about such things, Steppin, but if a man with as much experience as Mr. Cunningham is satisfied, I can't think you have any call to worry," Mrs. Stebbins consoled him.

"That's right, too," Steppin nodded. "But if you had been there and seen all that happened, you would worry, too."

When he got back to the theatre, just as he had expected, everything was in a state of confusion. The only thing that surprised him was the change in Mr. Cunningham. All his bad temper and blustering had vanished, and he fairly oozed confidence and good cheer.

"The house is sold out, and we are going to raise the curtain right on the dot," he told them. "We have a great little show and a top-notch cast, and as far as I can see, no one has a thing to worry about."

Steppin tried to feel reassured, but, in spite of himself, his mind kept harping back to the dismal failure of the last rehearsal. When the orchestra struck up in the stirring overture, his heart seemed to start beating louder and faster than the music.

"There I go," he groaned, "and here comes my old stage fright."

He tried to recall what Bob Williams had told him on the night of Dad Kirby's recital.

"That scared feeling does something for you, Steppin. It winds you up inside and makes you do your best. That's why a performance before an audience is always better than any rehearsal."

"Maybe that's why Mr. Cunningham is so sure we will do better than we did this afternoon," Steppin comforted himself. While the curtain was going up, it was so quiet you could have heard a pin drop. Then the lilting melody of the opening chorus burst forth, and the show was on.

Steppin, watching eagerly from the wings, felt his spirits soaring with the merry music. The chorus kept in a more perfect line than it had ever done at rehearsals, and above their beautiful costumes, the brown faces of the boys and girls were a sea of sparkling eyes and merry smiles. Steppin smiled to himself when he recalled how often at rehearsals Mr. Cunningham had threatened and implored them to keep their faces lifted.

One scene followed another without a hitch, and the play moved on as surely and brightly as a running brook.

"The Little Street in Harlem" scene in which Steppin made

his first appearance was a big number that came just before the intermission. As the curtain rose, several members of the chorus in colorful ragged clothes were promenading up and down a poor Harlem side street, while others were leaning out of the windows of a row of tenement houses. Sidney and another youngster were playing hopscotch on the street. Then, just as he had rehearsed it a hundred times, Steppin, turning slow cartwheels, came on and joined the two boys. A spotlight singled out Marcia Andrews, and she began singing "A Little Street in Harlem" in her deep, plaintive voice. The rest of the chorus strolled on and then everyone moved away from the center of the stage as Bob Williams, with his familiar derby and cane, strolled jauntily up to the footlights, with Roddy, a perfect copy of Bob, in step behind him.

Mr. Cunningham need have no fear that Steppin would forget himself and start daydreaming this time. Not one of all Bob's admirers in the big audience watched the dance with more rapt attention than did Steppin.

"Bob's as perfect as ever, and Roddy is just about as perfect," he observed as he tried to follow every single step of each dancer. "Roddy got a great chance, and he sure is making good.

"I don't envy him his part," Steppin decided. "It was coming to him, and he deserved it. But I sure would like to have just one chance to dance with Bob Williams before I die."

The tumult of applause that broke out when the dance was over ended all Steppin's doubts. He felt sure the play would be a success and would have a long run on Broadway.

"That's the way I feel, too," Roddy told him when they were talking things over, back in the dressing room. "I said as much to Bob, but he told me you never can be sure until you see what the critics write about it in the papers."

"Critics!" Steppin snorted. "If any of them have the nerve to take free tickets to a show as good as this and then not give it a good write-up, they ought to lose their jobs."

The next morning, when Steppin woke up, Mary Ellis had all the morning papers ready for him.

"Every single one of them says it is a wonderful play," she told him, and as he eagerly scanned the columns, he learned that she was right.

As he read and re-read every word of the reviews, he remembered what Mr. Cunningham had said about a show being built around a few great stars. Roddy's dancing received a few words of praise, and some of the other actors were mentioned favorably. But for the most part, all the glory went to Bob and Marcia, and the rest of them were described only as a fine supporting cast.

Now that the show was apparently settled for a long run in New York, Mr. Cunningham's chief worry was that one of the stars would get sick or that, worse yet, a star and his understudy would get sick at the same time. His first concern when the cast arrived at the theatre was to see that the stars were in sound health and that their understudies were on hand in case they were needed.

Sidney and Mrs. Ross seemed never to be able to get to the theatre on time, and often Roddy and Bob would be in the wings, waiting to go on before Sidney was ready. The cast became resigned to hearing Mr. Cunningham's nightly explosion when he found that Roddy's understudy was late.

In spite of Mr. Cunningham's worry, no serious illnesses occurred even among the less important members of the cast until just three weeks before the closing night. Then little Bernie Brown, who had been sniffling with a head cold, came down with a chill just before the Harlem street scene went on. The doctor, who was summoned, said Bernie was getting the measles and had him bundled up and sent home in a taxi. Except that Sidney had to play hopscotch alone, the scene went on as usual.

Steppin hated to think of the day when he would leave the show. It was going on the road, he knew, but Mr. Cunningham had explained to him that he was cutting down on the cast and only Roddy and Sidney would be taken along. However, he had made money and his mother had saved a good share of it.

"Even if I don't work again for a year, we will be all right," he thought with deep satisfaction.

Pretty soon it was his last week of the show, and then the last matinee, and finally one Saturday morning, when Steppin woke up, he thought, "Tonight will be my very last night."

At the theatre in the familiar bustle and excitement before the curtain rose, Steppin felt even more keenly the change that leaving the show would make in his life. He would miss Roddy a lot, too, he thought. Roddy also looked pretty glum, Steppin noticed when they were getting ready in their corner of the men's dressing room.

"Golly, Roddy, you have no call to look so down when you are going on with the show," Steppin told him.

"It's not that, Steppin." Roddy glanced around to make sure they were alone. "I feel something terrible," he confided.

"You mean you're sick?"

Roddy nodded miserably.

"It's been coming over me all last night and today. So far, I've kept it from my mother and Mr. Cunningham. I reckon I can carry through tonight all right, but I'm worried about whether I can go with the show tomorrow."

"You do look down at the gills, no fooling, and look, Roddy, you've got funny spots on your face, too."

Roddy leaned over and squinted into their mirror. "My head is thumping, and my eyes hurt so bad I can hardly see," he complained. "Do you think those spots will show from out front?"

Steppin backed away and was trying to decide how Roddy's speckled light-brown face and red-rimmed eyes would appear to the audience when Mr. Cunningham walked in. He took one look at Roddy.

"Jumping catfish," he exploded. "What's the matter with you, Roddy?"

"I'm all right," Roddy protested. "I've just got a cold or something."

"A cold! You look as if you had the smallpox. Here, lie down and cover up until we get the doctor. Poor kid, you're all shaking," Mr. Cunningham added with gruff kindness.

"Measles," Dr. Bemis announced after a brief examination. "Not a chance," to the director's eager inquiry as to whether Roddy could go on.

"Where is that Sidney Ross?" bellowed Mr. Cunningham, but as usual, Sidney and his mother were nowhere to be found.

"This is the last straw," Mr. Cunningham declared, pacing up and down and holding his head in his hands. "I'll fire that kid and his mother and break that contract if it's the last thing I ever do. Where is Bob?" and as Bob appeared at the doorway, "Roddy is sick, Bob, and you'll have to do the street scene number alone. It's a darn shame to have this happen on the last night too."

Roddy raised himself on his elbow.

"Mr. Cunningham," he said eagerly, "Steppin knows my dance as well as Sidney. He has gone through it with me lots of times. He could do it with Mr. Williams, if you would let him."

Mr. Cunningham looked doubtful.

"Do you think you could, Steppin?"

Steppin nodded solemnly. "I know I could do it."

"Why not try him out?" Bob suggested.

"Why not?" Mr. Cunningham agreed.

"Look, Bob, I'll have him go through it with Danny, and you can help me decide."

Danny was called, and Steppin fell into step behind him.

"Whether they let me do it or not, I'll still be in Roddy's favor if I live to be a hundred," Steppin thought as he concentrated on recalling every pose and gesture of the dance.

When he had finished, he knew even before they spoke that they were satisfied.

Bob and Mr. Cunningham were smiling broadly. Mr. Cunningham patted him on the back.

"Good boy, Steppin. That was great. And now if that Ross kid doesn't show up in five minutes, you win!"

"I reckon Mom would think I was pretty mean, but I sure hope whatever is keeping Sidney will keep him for five more minutes," thought Steppin as he wavered between hope and despair.

After what seemed an age, Mr. Cunningham ordered, "Get dressed, Steppin. It's all yours."

Mr. Cunningham made a few last-minute changes to cover the omission of the hopscotch playing and Steppin's cartwheels, and then, before Steppin had time to think, he was out on the stage, tapping, swinging his cane and tipping his derby in unison with his idol. Then, his long dreamed-of moment came, and he was stepping up to the footlights to take a curtain call with the great Bob Williams.

"Well, if there had to be a last night, it was great to have it go off with a bang," Steppin consoled himself when the show was over.

Everyone had been so kind and friendly and praised his dance so wholeheartedly that he hated more than ever to think of parting from the show. He had said "goodbye" to everyone and was just leaving when Mr. Cunningham called him back.

"Steppin, first I want to know just one thing, and that is, have you had the measles?" Mr. Cunningham asked.

"Yes, sir, I've had both kinds," Steppin assured him.

"Good!" Cunningham exclaimed. "Then you go home and pack up and be ready to leave with the show tomorrow."

Steppin's face lit up. "You mean you are going to let me go as Sidney's understudy?" he asked eagerly.

Mr. Cunningham looked at Bob, and they both grinned.

"Better than that, Steppin. You are going to take Roddy's place until he gets back. For once Mr. Cunningham misjudged Sidney. We've just heard he has the measles, too," Bob told him.

"Are you sure your mother won't put up any objections?"

Mr. Cunningham asked for the dozenth time as he was giving Steppin his orders.

"No, I'm sure Mom won't mind my going," Steppin assured him. "She'd never stand in my way if I wanted to do something that was right."

"Well, you'd better plan on quite a trip, Steppin, for if I know Mrs. Ross, the show will be closed before she'll think Sidney is able to work again, so when Roddy comes back, you will be his understudy in Sidney's place. And remember, in the meanwhile, you have no understudy, so for heaven's sake, don't come down with anything," Mr. Cunningham implored as they said goodnight.

"I'll sure try not to," promised Steppin. Bob Williams came out of his dressing room as Steppin was passing.

"I'll drive you uptown, Steppin," he offered kindly.

"Mr. Williams, if you gave me the car, after all that's happened to me tonight, I'd not have any more words to thank you," Steppin told him. "If Dad Kirby could see me now, he'd think my head was swelled for sure."

"You will have plenty of ups and downs in this profession," Bob prophesied. "Just now, you are up so you might as well enjoy it while you can. But don't expect it will always last, and when you come down, see that you take the bumps with a grin."

When Bob guided the car into Central Park, Steppin remembered clearly the first day he had met Bob and driven with him in that same park. And then he remembered how downhearted he had been as he sat on the hitching block before Bob drove up. He relaxed happily against the soft cushions and tapped his toes softly on the floor of the car. Then he hummed,

> "First I'm up and then I'm down,
> Now, I'm off for Cleveland town.
> Bumps may come, and bumps may go.
> But now I'm riding high, I know."

"Well, here we are, Steppin." Bob drew up to the curb at the corner and let Steppin out. "Good night, trouper," Bob called back as he drove off.

Steppin watched Bob's car until it drove out of sight.

"I hope Mom and Mary Ellis will still be up," he thought as he started for home. "If I have to wait until morning to talk to them, I'm like to bust."

When he sighted a light in their window, he broke into a run.

"Bumps may come, and bumps may go
But now I'm riding high, I know,"

he sang as he dashed down the steps three at a time and rushed into the house to tell them his wonderful news.

THE END

More Books from The Good and the Beautiful Library!

*The Golden Hawks of
Genghis Kahn*
by Rita Ritchie

*Harriet, the Moses of
Her People*
by Sarah H. Bradford

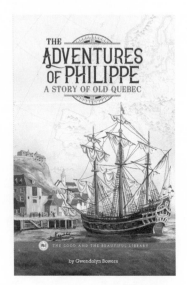

The Adventures of Philippe
by Gwendolyn Bowers

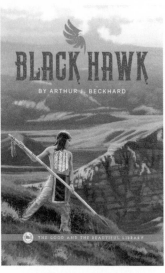

Black Hawk
by Arthur J. Beckhard